NO TIME LIMIT

Volume One

J. MICHAEL O'CONNOR

This book is dedicated to

My beloved son, Sean Patrick O'Connor

12.20.1976–10.02.2007

My adoring soul mate, Christine Jane

O'Connor

03.22.1951–11.25.2014

J. Michael O'Connor

Art design by J. Michael O'Connor

A special thank you to Mrs. Sharon Clevenger, in your celestial domain, for inspiring and encouraging me to write this entire story.

All names, characters, and incidents portrayed in this novel are fictional. Therefore, no identification with or similarity to actual persons, living or dead, or actual events is intended or inferred.

J. Michael O'Connor

Contents

It Begins

Two young boys were pretending to be Indiana Jones, the great explorer, in a large section of the forest not far from their homes, located in the eastern mountains of Tennessee. As they came down onto an old logging road, they saw a yellow compact two-door Volkswagen Golf parked within a half-mile of the end of the very rough logging road. Cautiously approaching the car, they crouched down and sneaked up on the car from the back, instantly shifting their imagination to the spy world of James Bond.

As the two boys eased up to the right side of the car and looked in from the right-rear window, which was splattered with blood, they saw the nude body slumped over toward the right side of the car. "Holy shit! Let's get out of here!" The ten-year-old proclaimed to his nine-year-old adventurous playmate. Quickly they ran to the nearest house, some two miles away. The older man who lived there had no phone but did have an old 1955 red Chevy pickup truck. The boys told the seventy-plus-year-old man what they had seen and asked him to take them down the mountain to a country store where they could call for help. He did, and the boy's parents and the county and state police arrived in a short time. Full rigor had set in, as it had been two days since Richard Finkel's sudden demise.

Narrator

His destiny lay with his students. He had no intentions of becoming a high school teacher, nor had his plans included moving to the Appalachian mountains of southwestern Virginia.

James Patrick O'Francis' gift was his ability to communicate with teenagers. He seemed to understand them better than most. He never breached their trust, nor did he ever betray their deepest secrets. He listened, counseled, and advised. He was even directly involved when requested. His teaching ability was not just the knowledge of the subject. It was his delivery. He made the subject easy for his students to understand the material. He required effort from each of them and a lot of it. It was said by many, "He was hard." I have learned from my sources, "hard," no; demanding, yes. To reach the zenith of an individual's ability to obtain knowledge. In addition, he made learning fun, and he had fun in his classes.

He enjoyed teaching, passing knowledge on to the students that graced his "think tank."

He believed he was directed to where he was for a reason. He often questioned why, but the answer always came back, "The students."

☿

It took years for James Patrick to put together the small, insignificant pieces of the giant puzzle of his life in a small, rural mountain community. He had been unable to see the big picture for years because he was so deep in the forest that he actually could not see the trees. In addition, his loyalty and devotion to a small high school program blinded him.

But in his defense, perception and deceit were everything. It ruled anything that had a political connection to it—large, medium, and tiny. The scale of politics was irrelevant; it was the same game.

Egos of men in power, and with power driving them, they befriend, betray, and cloak themselves in dishonor. Men who are dissembled are weak in character. Their mendacity was endless, and they were experts at the art of performing these qualities.

However, to tell James Patrick's story of his revenge for the character assassination he suffered, I will have to fill in a few gaps in his daily routine as a simple teacher.

He was slowly putting the little pieces of the puzzle of his life in a small, insignificant mountain town together. But when it was completed, and he stepped back to view the picture, his anger was overwhelming.

At this point in his story, I should add that people should always know who they are character assassinating. Because if the assassin does not know with whom they are dealing and to whom they have connections, one may find that it was not worth the small reward they had received for the price they would ultimately have to pay.

Tomorrow is promised to no one. In the real world, people are tortured, and people die. Most people live in a pretend world in the isolated world of education. But for those who have not had to endure the real world, the world in which they lived and felt they would always be safe and secure, was about to enter the world of harsh reality. An exclusive group of self-deemed important people who thought they were untouchable and could control everything in "their world" had hurt the wrong person.

Death is not such a bad thing. It is inevitable. It is the living who have to suffer. So, what is a good death? The answer should be any death that rids the world, society, community, town, city, or humanity of some form of human social disease. That should be defined as a good death. A good death is awarded to someone evil who, in the course of their existence, causes pain, suffering, misery, personal humiliation, character assassination, and heartache for some other human being.

However, most of society makes excuses for these types of people. Most of society reverts to the "Good Book" and its so-called good words to live by. The fractured fairy tale Book's worldwide circulation leads the mindless sheep with excuses for all evil beings. The "Book" has been cherry-picked over the centuries or altered to fit the editor's narrative and printed for the mass.

So, now you are asking yourself, what is this story about? It is about administering death to bad people and the justifiable reasons for doing so.

I am John Frederick O'Donovan, a freelance writer, and I have over many years traveling the world, writing down the stories about people whose paths I have crossed. I have seen and written about the suffering of humans caused by nature in its cruelest form and the evilness that exists on this earth. I have been very successful financially, and now I am semiretired and have been for several years. I settled in the Appalachian mountains of Eastern Tennessee in 1980 to write about the area's people and those who settled in the Appalachian Mountains of Southwestern Virginia, Southeastern Kentucky, and Western North Carolina. I wanted to write about the hard-working class of people who arrived in these areas and began carving out a meager living within the vast labyrinth of mountainous terrain and turned the area into a patchwork of productive, thriving small towns and communities.

This area had been part of a Native American hunting ground for seven tribes surrounding the forests and woodlands within a hundred or so miles radius. The Germans, Scotch, and Irish drove the Native Americans west, carving up the land into farms, vast areas of land that would become adjoining states. With the European invaders carving, cutting, and digging out a living over the past two hundred years, the forests had been raped, the land surface had been scarred, and the mountains had been gutted, leaving its underbelly hollow. This action caused the surface of the mountainous land in many places to collapse, destroying the underground water system and leaving hundreds of people high and dry.

I had no idea I would run across an Irishman with no connections to the area's earlier settlers and that I would become obsessed with his saga. We met at a social gathering, and after a brief conversation with James Patrick O'Francis, my journalistic instincts took over, and I was drawn to this person and the not-so-simple life he led. I decided to write about one man's fight against the injustices in a rural school system and the politically corrupt county where he resided. Unfortunately, his enduring effort to keep his surname intact and untarnished was a fight he would ultimately lose. His name and character would become tarnished by the callous, malicious, self-serving, self-righteous, dissembling, politically connected people of the county where he lived and worked, ultimately driving him out of the mountains he so loved.

After several years of following O'Francis throughout his somewhat normal life of being a simple high school teacher and learning of his past as well as his philosophies, he walked out of my life on a cool August night, fog encircling the mountain midway down to the valley floor like a ring of Saturn. The night sky was filled with the celestial twinkling of millions of tiny lights as we looked out over a white cloud ringing my mountain sanctuary. He had a few simple words, "There is no time limit," and then he turned and walked away, got in his Jeep, and drove off, disappearing into the midst of a white cloud of fog.

I grew to know James Patrick after several years of research and private conversations.

He had a pure spirit and enjoyed many genres of music. James was very artistic and craved adventure. In addition, he strived to be a good-natured person.

James liked to put others before himself. He loved nature and wanted to be outside most of the time. James also had a fierce side to him, but only to the people who deserved it. He had trust issues because he had been betrayed and hurt many times. James Patrick was not a religious man, yet he believed in a spiritual existence. He had a great sense of humor. He could be extremely tender when he wanted to.

The last I saw of him, James was a broken man. The once bright light that had pierced his darkened world and made it shine for years had suddenly and unexpectedly gone out. His beloved Dawn was all that kept him balanced. His loss turned him bitter toward life itself. Darkness once again overshadowed his world.

As I sit on my upper deck, looking out over the hardwood-laden mountain in reflection, his voice echoing the words that come back to me loud and clear, I see him walking off into the darkness of the night. Several years have passed, and I once again find myself drawn like a moth to a bright light to investigate the connections between the events that have occurred over the past few years and the man I knew as James Patrick O'Francis.

He was a man of his word. I know that. He was a man of honor, a man out of his time. He was a man who wanted to be left alone to live the life of a simple teacher, build a home for his adoring wife, and raise his beloved sons in a safe, clean environment. But unfortunately, the people who had forced the changes in his life had no idea what Pandora's box held in it.

He often said he did not like reporters, especially media reporters, as he felt they had no honor and were rude and interruptive. They were not without malice in any story they were reporting. After some event was reported on television, he often told me that the report was done without caring about whom the story was being told. All they cared about was the ratings they would get. Ratings equated to money, and that was what it was all about and nothing else. They couldn't care less about the people the story was being reported about; whether it was accurate was not the case. Get the ratings up. If it turned out that it was not correct, maybe one would see or hear a minor blip about the correction, and they would move on to some other so-called truth that had to be reported: "Because it was the right of the people to know."

"Yeah, right," he would always say. "Right of the people, my ass."

However, James did give journalists and the general media a sizeable edge over politicians. Over the years of talking with him, I found he loathed almost all politicians. The oddity was that James loved to study politics and was quite the expert on our political system. However, he would often remind me that he did not like reporters. Then he would get a big smile on his face.

Looking back on my relationship with James P. and being a journalist, I do not know why he agreed to talk. Nevertheless, he slowly and cautiously kept meeting with me and answering my many questions. I tried to be honest, and he tested me many times. Maybe he kept meeting with me because of the location of my home, the remote isolation, and the purity of the land surrounding it. He told me many times that he always wanted to live on a mountain without neighbors. Isolated and close enough to civilization, he and Dawn could enjoy modern-day social conveniences and escape back to his mountaintop sanctuary.

Maybe he kept returning because of the fate topic we often discussed. But he always reminded me, "You know, John, nothing happens out of just coincidence."

I do not know. However, I do know that the cost to James P. would be more than he could take, and in the end, his dark side took over. His Celtic characteristics of seeking revenge on those who harmed his family would rule and guide his fate. The cry of the banshee would be heard.

I have learned that the events that led to his departing his beloved Appalachian Mountains and the events that occurred sometime after he left the area are so unbelievable that I have decided to continue with the saga of James Patrick O'Francis.

Justice Awakens

I had not seen James Patrick in many years, and I realized as I sat on my back upper deck, my feet laid out on the wicker ottoman. I was reading the Sunday paper, not absorbing anything I was reading. I turned one page after another, skimming one article after another, sipping my coffee, and enjoying the warm eight o'clock rays. The spring birds were singing, and Boaz, my very large cat, had his front paws turned inward, purring contentedly on my lap. Then, an article on the front page flashed through my mind again. I quickly turned back to the front page and scanned through several stories, and there in the right-hand column, midway down the page with a medium headline, was a short article that had subconsciously caught my attention. *A teacher was found dead in his car.*

The article did not give many details concerning the death, but the name that stood out in my memory was Richard Finkel.

I decided to do some investigating that day, as I had learned a lot about that particular person and several others who had been a large part of a conspiracy to destroy the character and career of J. Patrick O'Francis.

I remembered O'Francis' last few years and what drove him to leave the southwest Virginia Appalachian Mountains. I needed my file on Jim, so I lifted Boaz off my lap, placing him on the decking, much to his dislike, as he informed me with a disapproving meow. I refilled my morning coffee, returned to my favorite chair, and sat on the deck to review the O'Francis file from that August night when he walked out of my life, covering his last fifteen years. A lot had happened to him in his previous fifteen years. Almost as much as in his first twenty. I learned a lot about this simple teacher who was not so simple. I mentally reminded myself, as I began reviewing, that I did not have his complete story. A lot of pieces were missing.

Friday after school was the last time anyone saw Mr. Richard Finkel as he did his usual come-ons and fraternization with the young seventeen- and eighteen-year-old girls in the back parking lot. The eighteen-year-old he was seducing, and the two seventeen-year-old girls were on his schedule to be violated and placed on his trophy wall.

The girls walked off toward their cars, and Richard smiled and informed them he would see them later. He got into his car and started it when a black four-door Chrysler 300 pulled crossways behind Finkel's car, preventing him from backing up. The two men in the back of the Chrysler got out and casually walked to the driver's door of Richard's car. He looked up at the two well-dressed men in navy-blue pinstriped suits, white shirts, and expensive silk ties.

"Mr. Richard Finkel?" one of the men asked.

"Yeah, what can I do for you?" Finkel responded in his usual cocky, ill-mannered tone.

"Would you please step out of the car? There is someone who would like to talk to you."

Finkel had become instantly irritated; however, for whatever reason, a slight quiver in his inner self occurred, brought on by the deep, unfeeling business tone of the voice coming from the man facing him.

Richard asked, "Who is it?"

The two huge men just asked him to please step out of the car as one reached down and opened the driver's door for Finkel.

Richard unbuckled his seat belt and swung his legs around, placing his feet on the ground.

He looked up at the men positioned themselves on either side of him. As he stood, his midsection began to tremble again as both expressionless men towered some five inches over him and outweighed him by twenty-five pounds of solid, well-developed physique.

The man on his right laid his hand toward the black Chrysler with the right-rear door open, indicating for him to get into the car. Richard hesitated momentarily and then made the mistake of looking into the man's eyes at his left. He saw cold, dark, hard, steel-gray eyes, and a cold surge traveled up Richard's back, leaving a broad trail of bumps. He nodded his head and did as the two men asked.

Finkel's involvement in illegal gambling, drug contacts, being the drop-off for drug dealers, and his distribution to lower-rung dealers as an intermediary, the go-between at a public school, had never stopped since his departure from Honsburg High School many years earlier. His position as athletic director at the school he worked in after his requested resignation at Honsburg again allowed him to communicate and contact an extensive range of diverse and somewhat unscrupulous people better location than the rural school in Honsburg. The city school allowed for more accessible and discreet connections for his illegal product delivery and a good place for somebody to come by and pick up the products.

Finkel was well paid for his little service by a much larger organization. However, his usual tough persona and arrogant image in and around Vermillion High School had suddenly wilted in the presence of the men he now faced. As Richard got into the back seat of the Chrysler, the man standing at Richard's little yellow Golf pulled a pair of rubber gloves out of his suit pocket and placed them on his hands. He then wiped the door handle with a clean white cloth, where he had put his hand to open it. He then got into Richard's automobile. The man who escorted Richard to the Chrysler closed the door after Finkel had gotten into the Chrysler, and then he walked around to the rear driver's side of the car and got in. There were two men in the front seat. The driver pulled slightly forward; the man on the passenger's side looked toward Richard's car, nodded, and pulled out with Finkel's car following.

"Excuse me. But why is that man driving my car?"

No one spoke. Again, Finkel said, "I asked you a question. Could someone tell me what is going on?"

The man to his left spoke. His voice had a deep, rough tone to it. "Just sit where you are and shut your mouth."

The drive took forty-five minutes, leaving the city and traveling into the countryside on a narrow, isolated road. Finally, the black Chrysler 300 pulled in behind a dark-gray Jeep Grand Cherokee parked on a wide spot on the isolated rural country road. Finkel had asked who they were and what they wanted several times and got no response from any three men. The music playing in the Chrysler was a selection of the best of the Eagles.

The man in the back with Richard got out, walked to Richard's door, opened the door, and asked him to get out. Finkel had turned as pale as any Caucasian could have turned, and sweat was running down his face as fear permeated his eyes. He was escorted to the Jeep and placed on the left side of the back seat. The other man on the front passenger's side of the Chrysler got out and got behind the Jeep's steering wheel. Finkel then panicked and attempted to get out of the back of the Jeep. The steel-gray-eyed man was at the rear door of the Jeep, where he met Finkel with a fist to his mouth, sending him stumbling back into the Jeep. He shoved his legs into the Jeep, closed the door, walked around to the passenger's door, and got into the front seat. He pulled out a pistol with a silencer attached, turned slightly to his left, pointed the pistol at him, and ordered, "Now you sit there like a good little boy."

The Jeep pulled out with Finkel's yellow Golf following, and the Chrysler turned and went in the opposite direction. The Jeep went deeper into the mountains, driving from the paved road to a gravel road to a dirt road to an old unused logging road, where the Jeep pulled over just enough for the Golf to get by and then proceeded to the near end of the road. It had been a rather steep grade, and the Golf had difficulty making it, bottoming out several times and spinning the tires to get up the rough, rutted-out road.

They came to a stop on a level area of about a hundred feet square on the logging road and proceeded to pull Richard Finkel out of the back of the Jeep, his mouth still bleeding as one of the men walked him to the left of the Jeep and instructed him to remove all his clothes. He refused, and a fist to the side of his jaw put him on the ground, semiconscious. Then two of the three men removed all his clothes and placed them in a plastic bag, leaving him naked from head to toe. The steel-gray-eyed man removed his suit coat and rolled his shirtsleeves up to his elbows.

"Mr. Finkel," he stated, "you no doubt question why you find yourself in such an awkward position."

Richard began crying as he rolled over and came to his knees, bending at his waist, looking up at all three men surrounding him.

"No, no, I don't. I, I, I don't even know you guys. I have done nothing to you. What is this about? I don't understand. You must have the wrong person."

"Now, Richard, you know!"

"No, no, no, I really don't." He sobbed some more.

"Let me refresh your memory just a little." The well-groomed, steel-gray-eyed man spoke in his deep voice. "Do you remember what you and others like you have done to a very close friend of ours? Now, I know you have damaged many people with your mouth. But, this one particular person, you took part in destroying his career and tainting his character!"

Richard Finkel paused momentarily in deep thought. He had, over the years, been a part of the destruction of at least four teachers' careers, not excluding the many cases of sexual violations of teenage girls in three different schools. Then, he began making statements that he was never in charge, just doing what he was told, and meant no harm. Richard had no clue which one of the teachers the men were talking about.

"Let me help you a little, Mr. Finkel. Did you ever work at a high school called Honsburg?"

"Yes," came a meek reply. Then came the naming of people, spilling his guts freely, claiming he was only following their instructions.

At that, one of the men grabbed him by the hair and pulled him back hard onto the ground, forcing his hands onto the ground above his head, placing his knees on the open palms of each hand. The other man grabbed his feet and spread-eagled him on the ground. As the steel-gray-eyed man put his rubber gloves on, he spoke.

"Mr. Finkel, how many little girls have you raped?"

"What? None, I swear. None really." His voice was trembling with each word.

"Now, Mr. Finkel, you mean to lie here in your state and confess to us you have never seduced any teenagers?"

Richard responded quickly, thinking they had the wrong man with that statement. "No, no, no, I have never raped any teens." Finkel was looking up at the man with the rubber gloves on.

"You lie there naked and tell me you have never had sex with any teenager in any high school you have ever worked at?"

"Ahhh, well, I ...."

The man standing above him cut him off. "Now, don't lie to me!" His voice was hard and stern.

"I mean, I have had a few, but they were not raped."

The man removed a scalpel with a number 12 blade from a black leather case, curved precisely for the job to be performed, and then proceeded to castrate Richard Finkel. Richard opened his mouth to scream, and just as he did, a clean white cloth was placed into his mouth, muffling the sounds. The man with the scalpel then cut his penis off, holding them in his left hand, showing them to Finkel. Richard's eyes were as wide as a human could have been, still groaning from the sudden shock to his body. The man leaned down close to Richard's face and said, "Don't guess you will be fucking any more teens!"

Then he placed his bloody manhood on his bare chest. He reached down and quickly removed the cloth from his mouth as Finkel began to scream, and with the skill of a surgeon, he grabbed Finkel's tongue with a pair of ten-inch stainless-steel curved hemostats and, with the scalpel, cut Finkel's tongue out, placing it on Finkel's chest.

Before Richard lost consciousness, the man spoke in a deep, unfeeling voice. "You will never again speak evil of our friend's good name!" Finkel began choking on his blood as it drained down his throat. The steel-gray-eyed man then pulled off his gloves and placed them into the plastic bag with Richard's other clothes. He cleaned the scalpel and hemostat with a clean white alcohol-soaked cloth and put each back into the leather case. Next, he walked to the Jeep's hood, where he had laid his coat. He placed the case in the inside pocket of his suit coat. He then put the bloody cloth he had cleaned the scalpel into the bag with the rest of Finkel's attire. The two other men were getting Finkel to his feet, the extracted parts of his body dropping to the ground. Dragging Finkel to his car, blood dripping from his mouth and groaning, they placed him in the driver's seat. The seat had been moved back as far as it would go, and the back had been tilted halfway back to allow for ease of placing Finkel's now very limp body into the driver's seat. Two men returned to the Jeep, got into the front seat, and started the engine.

The man with the cold, steel-gray eyes then pulled out a pistol with a silencer on it. He calmly walked to the driver's door of the yellow Golf, pointed it toward Finkel's left temple, and popped the cap, splattering Richard's skull, blood, and brains all over the passenger's side of the interior of his car. The man calmly walked back to the driver's door of the Jeep, pausing momentarily to replace a clean pair of rubber gloves on his hands, and the man behind the steering wheel of the Jeep handed him a dark-purple lily wrapped in green wrapping paper. He went to where his manly parts had fallen to the ground, picked them up, returned to Finkel's car, and placed the lily, minus the paper, on Richard's bloody, nicked lap. He tossed his penis, testicles and tongue on the floor at Finkel's feet. He then closed the door. He walked back to the Jeep, pulled his rubber gloves off, placed them in the plastic bag, picked his suit coat off the hood, put it on, set the bag in the back cargo compartment of the Jeep, and got into the back seat behind the driver. They left.

I had a few friends in the newspaper business, so I placed a call to one of them.

"*Bastally Daily Chronicle*, may I help you?"

"Good morning. May I speak to Ted West or Anthony Krause, please?"

"One moment, please." Several seconds went by as my call was transferred.

"Ted West here. May I help you?"

"Ted, this is John O'Donovan."

"Hey, what's up this bright, sunny morning? Got a good story for me, you old, retired dog?"

"Well, not really. I do not think. I need some information from you first. What do you know about the Finkel story?"

Ted paused, trying to remember what they had gathered from the Finkel story. Then he told me the bits and pieces of a story he had gathered, letting me in on as many details as they had, as he did owe me several favors. He informed me that he had gotten what he could from several teachers at the school where Finkel worked.

"Several students gave me a little information, but not much. But, of course, they were rather shaken up. But I guess that is understandable."

"Ted, how old were the students you talked to?"

There was a pause for several seconds. "I really don't know."

"Well, give me your best guess. And were they male or female?"

"Well, both."

"So how old, would you say?"

"Well, I would say...well, given their build, ohhh, seventeen or eighteen, maybe a few sixteen-year-olds. Why do you ask?"

"Oh, something I heard."

"What? Something I can use?" Ted quickly responded.

"Well, maybe, later. I want to check some of my facts out first."

As Ted and I continued their short conversation, Ted remembered the name of James Patrick O'Francis and a civil trial that had taken place several years earlier. Of course, the question any good newspaper reporter would ask, he asked: "John, do you think that O'Francis had anything to do with the torture and murder?"

I proceeded to inform Ted that I did not think so. I told him that O'Francis had moved from the area some years ago, and to my knowledge, no one had heard or seen him since.

Of course, Ted wanted to know where he was, and I told him I had no clue. The truth of the matter was that I really did not know for sure. Of course, I was lying about the fact that I didn't have a clue, as I had given my word, a "Brotherhood's" word. That meant everything to James Patrick.

As my mind flashed back to our last few conversations, I wondered if he and his Master had come to terms with what justice was.

Was this just a case of a corrupt teacher getting his just dues by any number of people connected to the illegal businesses, or maybe an enraged father?

The investigation revealed that there were traces of cocaine in the trunk of Finkel's car. The police concluded that he had been involved in drugs, had double-crossed someone, and paid the price.

Of course, the school's administrative personnel pretended that they had no clues about his corrupt character or that he had been involved in any wrongdoing. But, of course, they also did not know anything in his past that suggested he was involved in anything illegal. Finkel had been smooth, and they may have been semi-innocent, but not completely. Money can and did buy off a lot of people and have them look the other way. "I have no knowledge" comments became a well-known saying among many school administrators throughout the entire area. It was also known that most, not all, but most administrators from any surrounding school systems were like most politicians, liars, and cheats, not to discount, corrupt.

The phone tree had started throughout Reynolds County. Damon Bales now lived in the Abetton area and called Irvin Brewer first, who also moved to the lake area not far from Abetton. He then called LaMar Marshy, who had moved on to a county in the middle of the state, doing what he did best. Finally, the phone rang at Judge Danial Edwin's residence and the eight others who were the principal conspirators in destroying James Patrick O'Francis' career. Bales made an effort to connect with the county sheriff's department. However, a new sheriff was now in charge of the county, one with honor and integrity, Sidney Delta. He had cleaned up all but a few of the corrupt deputies within the department and worked on cleaning out the few remaining suspected corrupt members of his department.

Damon's panic resulted in a call to their connection with the state police, who was now retired. Panic had overtaken Damon, as he was the most paranoid of all the people connected to O'Francis' past. He quickly found nothing could be done about what he perceived as happening. Damon and Brewer had tried to get the county commonwealth attorney (also new to the county and one with a degree of honor), as well as the sheriff's department, to issue a warrant for James Patrick, as that was whom they had automatically targeted as doing the "number" on Richard. That failed, as there was nothing of substance to their erroneous allegations. They could not get help from the state police because they had nothing connecting the accused person. They could not get any help issuing a warrant for James Patrick from the adjoining counties' legal and law-enforcement agencies (where the crime occurred), as no one knew who or where James Patrick was. And no one had any proof he was involved, which created more panic for the guilty-minded jackals who remained in Reynolds County.

All anyone in law-enforcement agencies had was some individual finger-pointing by this small group, and their power structure did not extend far outside their domain. Moreover, most of the finger-pointing people were well known for their tainted characters and methods of operation, and little credence was given to their accusations outside Reynolds County.

Sheriff Delta and several of his deputies, who had been students of O'Francis', talked among themselves, smiling at the possibility of O'Francis being the judge, jury, and executioner. Although they all were honorable police officers, one officer stated in the closed-door gathering, "Does my heart good to think that O'Francis pulled this off. Even though I do not think he is anywhere around this area to administer the due justice."

I decided to contact a few of my reliable sources. In doing so, I learned of "finger-pointing" and phone calls. I laugh at the reaction of Finkel's demise. The self-deemed importance of the group. The suffering they caused O'Francis and his family over the years. He was dealing with P.T.S.D. and all the mental duress that goes with it. I did not doubt that he could have performed such an act. However, I had gotten the impression from several of our talks that he may have had sources in places with great power and many tentacles that reached far and wide. Something else I learned about the people who had cut his career short with their iniquities: they did not know who they were dealing with. He once told me, "*Celts are not to be fucked with.*" Then he laughed.

Demotion

It was to be another year of heartache for O'Francis, as he started his year of teaching. He had been demoted to the lowest grade level Marshy and Damon could place him, the middle school. His stress level was once again reaching the high-level mark with the thoughts of working for someone who, years earlier, did everything he could to destroy his career. Yet, his emotions were like an EKG charted heartbeat. He was joyfully happy and at peace teaching the children that graced his "Think Tank." If the current administration and the central office "henchmen" would leave him along to teach. Now, once again, he faced working for his old nemesis Bobby Simms, the man who claimed he had done nothing to supplant O'Francis in the community, county, or school system. Like the small-town politician he was, the words he uttered were no different from someone on the national stage. Meaningless and often damaging to one's character and with malice.

His first day started with a faculty meeting where he knew no one, as Simms introduced O'Francis to the teachers. J. Patrick O'Francis' name was well known, with the "have you heard," and "did you know" gossip and whispers among the faculty members at Honsburg Elementary and Middle School. However, none knew the man. A formal meeting, many papers handed out telling you everything from when to go and not go, the times of duties, and dates. As O'Francis surveyed the room of mostly female teachers, he began feeling apprehensive as though an enemy he could not kill surrounded him.

Then, at the end of the forty-five-minute meeting, a woman of many years in teaching stood and stated, "I would like to tell everyone here that I am delighted that Mr. O'Francis is here at our school. I feel that he will make a much-needed addition to the faculty. I have heard that he is an excellent teacher. I think it is about high time we get quality teachers here at this school."

O'Francis did not know who the woman was and gave little value to her words, although the comments were very much appreciated. He had become 100 percent distrustful of all people, more especially anyone within the Reynolds School System.

As the meeting adjourned, Simms asked O'Francis to come to his office. *Such a formulary sound*, he thought. He had come to hate the words.

It was the same setting, just a different school. Simms sat behind his desk, Jim in one of two chairs in the room with the door closed. The only real exception was that Decal was not attached to Simms's hip.

"Mr. O'Francis, I feel that we need to talk. I hope that you and I can put all the past behind us and start over on a clean slate."

Jim sat taking notes on his legal pad. He had forgotten his tape recorder, as he had not expected to be in the principal's office so soon. *My bad,* he thought. *I will not make that mistake again.*

Simms paused momentarily and then continued, "I truly am glad you are here at this school. I am aware that you are an outstanding teacher. You know I have always said that. I feel we can have a good and productive year."

He went through all the rules and policies he had and then asked if Jim had any questions or needed anything.

James O'Francis was very polite and very professional. "No, sir, I do not think so at this time. I will adhere to all policies, rules, and regulations here at this school. I do want to be left alone to teach the children. I do not think that is too much to ask."

Simms stood, as did James O'Francis. He walked around the desk and extended his hand. Jim had a moment of hesitation, and then with great reluctance, Jim shook Simms's hand. He hated shaking someone's hand. For Jim O'Francis, it was a meaningless gesture.

"Now, Mr. O'Francis, you know that you and I have a common foe, don't you?" Their hands parted as O'Francis did not respond.

"You know," Simms continued. Jim's eyes were locked on Simms.

His insides were tense. His anxiety level had risen; his arms and hands felt warm. His mind raced at lightning speed. *I know too much about too many people. I do not trust you and no one else within the system in which I have to work. Damn, I just need to start fresh, even if I have been demoted. I am a teacher, a real teacher. I love teaching, and I love spreading knowledge that I hope will grow exponentially in all my students. Damn, I need for you and the rest of the jackals of the possessed demoniacs of chthonic to leave me the fuck alone.*

Bobby tried once again to get Jim to state a name. At that moment, he did not know who their common foe was. Several names instantly flashed through his mind: *Marshy, Bales, Finkel, Jones, Decal, Harper, good God, I did not think we had any common foe ... who is he referring to?* Jim was not trying to come up with a name. He only wanted to get out of the office of the enemy he was now in the presence of and could not do a damn thing to him.

"Sure you do," Simms stated as O'Francis stood in silence, looking directly into his eyes. "The man over in the central office," Simms said.

Jim did not comment. "Marshy. You know what he has done to you, and you know he and I do not join at the hip."

James Patrick thought as he stood looking directly at Bobby Simms, still not speaking. *No, but I damn sure know that you and Decal did a hell of a number on me over the years. In this glorious county as well as outside the county! He sure was joined at the hip with you.* Jim broke eye contact and looked at his watch on his left wrist.

"I've got to go, Mr. Simms, if there is nothing else, sir."

"No, no, I don't think so." Simms broke a big, warm smile. "Now, Mr. O'Francis, if you need anything, you just come see me."

J. Patrick made a sharp pivoting right and walked out of the office without anything else being said. As O'Francis walked the very long hallway toward his new classroom, which was the last classroom at the far end of the hall of the junior high section of the building, a song began to play in his mind. *"Smiling faces, smiling faces, tell lies, and I got the proof ... the evil that lurks within ... the truth is in the eyes, cause the eyes don't lie." Damn, the Temptations sure as fuck had that song right.*

River Fishing

It had been a rather stressful day, and James P. needed somewhere to go to think, somewhere alone, somewhere no humans would be. He did not feel like journeying to the mountains. His other retreat over the years, weather permitting, was the river.

Jim changed into his tan wading shorts, his green-and-gold pullover T-shirt with a football and golden helmet on the front with the words in the background, Notre Dame, in large letters. Across the middle of the back of his T-shirt were the words WE ARE ND in large letters. It was not as if anyone who ever knew him did not already know where his feelings lay. His loyalty never wavered in the good years or lean years. He was ND through and through. Putting his pocketknife in his left hip pocket, he went to his hat tree and picked his boonie hat off the rack, placed it on his head, his favorite for fishing as well as his mountain retreats. Then he picked a pair of white ankle-high socks out of his dresser drawer as he went out of the bedroom and down the hallway. He slipped on his flip-flops as he went through the utility room and went to his shed, "the barn," as he called it because it was shaped like a barn. He picked up his white low-cut tennis shoes that he wore each time he went fishing, took his fishing jacket off the hook he always hung it up on, reached up and retrieved his spinning reel and rod off its hanger he had made for the eight rods and reels, three of which were his youngest son's. He put all his fishing items in the truck bed, went back into his house, picked up a bottle of water, kissed Dawn, told her that he loved her, and went out the front door. Dawn told Jim to be careful, and Jim replied as he always did.

"If I die, make damn sure the damn insurance company does not screw you out of your money, and they will if they can. But hell, you know that they are nothing but legalized racketeers supported by the damn corrupt politicians anyway."

James P. started his truck and drove out of the driveway. Ten minutes later, he arrived at the river where he wanted to fish for the next three hours. He parked his truck some twenty yards down from the little church that sat several hundred feet above the river as it turned down the high cliffs that extended south above the little white church. Jim sat on the tailgate, putting on his socks and tennis shoes. Then he reached into the right upper pocket, one of the many pockets on his fishing jacket, and took out a pack of sugar-free chewing gum. Next, he took out two sticks, removed the wrappers, put the wrappers in a plastic trash bag he kept in the cab of his truck, placed the gum in his mouth, and chewed them for a few minutes as he put his rod together and put one of his Rebel crawfish on the end of his yellow line. James P. then took out a pack of Beechnut chewing tobacco and put a handful into his left jaw, mixing it with the gum he had gotten juicy.

Turning toward the river, he began his walk down the riverbank. Walking through the waist-high grasses and what he referred to as "hog weeds" for about one hundred yards, he came upon a red iron six-foot-long, four-foot-high farming gate. He opened it and passed to the other side, closing and latching the gate as he found it. He crossed over into a pasture area along the river with a tractor road that led along the riverbank. Jim continued to walk for half a mile down the river. He stopped and looked out at the shoals.

"Good spot to start," he stated aloud as if he was talking to someone present. Jim spit his mouthful of amber to his right and then stepped into the cool waters of the Clinch River.

The water was only a little above his ankles, with a rocky bottom of small rocks, the kind that is easy to walk on. He took several steps toward the middle of the river as the water's depth became deeper, up to the top of his knees. Finally, he stopped and cast his line toward the center of the swift-moving water.

Jim traversed the small and large rocks of the Clinch, occasionally losing his balance, and ended up sitting down in the river with the waters swirling around his upper body and over his shoulders. Regaining his balance in the swift-flowing water, he stood in thigh-high water, laughing at himself. Then he spit the tobacco juice into the water. He cast his line to the right side of the rocky shoals into a pool of bubbling oxygen-filled water at the far end, over the rocks that were protruding above the water, in hopes of catching the big bass of the day. Several casts into the same general spot, and he finally got a hit on the crawfish. His rod bent drastically toward the water below him as his line stretched tight, and he strained at the fish on the end of it.

Slowly he reeled the bass toward him. As the fish came over the rocky shoals, it broke the water's surface to free itself. The bass fought hard, and Jim gradually reeled it toward him. Now only ten yards away, the rod trembled as the large bass fought even harder. Jim reeled the big bass slowly to within two feet of himself and lifted the two-pound fish out of the water. He put his left thumb into the bottom of the bass's mouth, curling his index finger around his lower mouth. Placing his reel between his upper thighs, he reached into his left upper pocket, released the surgical hemostat, and removed the hooks from the bass's mouth. Holding the two-pound bass up, looking at it for a moment, Jim smiled, bent over, and released the fish back into the river to be caught yet another day, stating to the bass as if he could hear him, "Until next time, big boy."

Jim walked over a mile down the middle of the river, fishing from one side or the other, falling only once, with a couple of slips but regaining his balance. He had caught ten fish of various sizes, all bass. The beauty of the sun setting to his west and the glimmer of the reflection of the sun off the bubbling waters that flowed over and gushed between the rocks and boulders caused James Patrick to pause and lose himself in its beauty and sound. The temperature was still in the low eighties at six o'clock in the evening. All he could hear was the roar of the rushing water and the sound of a crow off toward the farmland that joined the river at its banks. Twenty yards to his right front stood a four-and-a-half-foot-tall blue crane at the edge of the water. Then out of the sky from behind Jim and thirty feet over his head, four wild ducks passed over him, landing a good fifty yards down the river to his front in the smoother, deeper waters. All with the grace of a navy pilot landing a Tomcat on the deck of a carrier.

To his left, the land's topography rose quickly and was covered with the hard woods of the southwestern part of the state. To his right, cattle grazed in the open fields that ran to the river's edge. He stood motionless with his reel and rod in his hand, poised to cast his line just across the top of the outcropping of rocks protruding above the water, where he thought would be a good place for yet another large bass. He stood immobile at the edge of yet another rocky shoal, looking down the river, the sun warm on his face. His clothes from his beltline up had dried to a very light dampness. His world began to move in slow motion as he just stood in the middle of the river gazing down toward the ducks. He was hearing nothing as his mind slipped into a far-off land in a far-off time.

The Creek

Rusty, Bill, Jim, and three "yards" loaded onto the chopper at 0500 hours for a trip into the forbidden jungle, as Jim often referred to it. Once again, the patrol was to infiltrate the domain of "Charlie," gather information on his activities and then report their findings to Captain Thompson, who would pass it along to the SOG officer, who would do whatever with it. Then, most likely, Jim figured after all the "brains" mulled over the Intel, they would be tapped for a major ambush patrol.

The taxi pilots were always in a joking mood, which Jim liked, and yet he did not like it as he was never in the mood for wisecracks and jokes when flying out on a mission, yet Rusty was always telling him to lighten up, that everything was going to be okay. Sometimes Jim thought his closest friend was hiding his fears behind his ever-optimistic approach to missions like the one they were embarking upon. Jim was in no mood, especially that early in the morning, for chopper pilot wisecracks. But, deep down, he knew they only did it to take the tension off the mission. Jim knew the pilots knew the dangers, not only to the patrol but also to themselves.

They were as good at their job as Jim, and the members of the patrols were at their jobs. They were also a part of a very elite group of men who were placed in harm's way on a near-daily basis. Their performance under fire could not be matched, and the lives they saved in the heat of a firefight were beyond heroic. As far as Jim was concerned, when he had been pulled out of a compromised mission, the pilots should have been given the Congressional Medal of Honor on more than one occasion.

As I have learned over the many conversations with him, he did not believe in medals and glorifications or been put on some front-page story about anything he did while simply doing his job. His job, just like thousands of other combat soldiers have done.

But be that as it may, the pilots were at their best. Of course, Jim did not laugh; Bill and Rusty did, and the "yards" did not get the humor to start with, so they were as poker-faced as Jim. Jim got to know the pilots well, and they got to know him. He was not always as hard-faced toward their humor, just on specific missions, which led to locations he was not happy about going into.

It was not that any places were good places to go, but some were far worse than others. Jim hated the location where they were going. Nothing ever seemed to work out correctly in that particular part of the jungle, AO (area of operation). Moreover, this jungle area was an area they had never reconned, and they knew nothing about it other than what the maps showed them.

The flight did not last all that long, thirty minutes, but one can cover a lot of terrain in a chopper within thirty minutes. The geographic location put the "green taxi" down on a small hill with a clearing just large enough for one Huey to hover six feet off the ground. The patrol was out and clear within seconds, and the ever-dependable UH-1 Iroquois was lifting above the trees and slanting off to the east by the time the patrol set up under the thick canopy.

As Jim lay motionless, listening to the sounds of the surrounding jungle and its ever-present noises, the birds and other assorted species returned to their morning wake-up calls after being disturbed by the deep popping sound of the Huey's large blades cutting through the early morning air. O'Francis carefully surveyed the area. Not seeing anything at any distance made him uneasy about this patrol. His thoughts were on the patrol's name, "Cripple Creek." *Jesus Christ, why in the hell did the "old man" let Billy call it Cripple Creek? Shit, only a boy from the mountains of North Carolina with the nickname of Hawk would do that. Bill thought it was funny. Oh, just like the song, he said. Fuck a bunch of songs; bad name for a patrol like this one in this area. All because the topo map showed that we had to descend into and travel down a fucking creek.* Then the frigging song started going over and over in his mind.

"Going down Cripple Creek, going on the run, going down Cripple Creek, going to have me some fun ..." Geez, bluegrass. Damn, I hate bluegrass. What was it Hawk said? Oh yeah, "Bill Monroe is the greatest."

Ten minutes passed, and the Cripple Creek Patrol gathered and began their descent toward the creek. It was approximately one klick (0.62 miles) straight down the mountain, so the map showed. Going straight was out of the question.

After meandering for two hours at a snail's pace through thick jungle foliage, making little or no noise to reach the upper headwaters of the creek, Hawk held up his left arm. His fist clenched high in the air to the man behind him. The man behind him repeated the same sign and the man behind him until all had frozen in place. Finally, they had reached the creek. A steep ninety-degree bank at least seven feet high lay before them as they dropped into the calf-high water one by one. According to the map, it appeared they had connected to the creek about a third of the way from its alleged headwaters. Jim was unsure how far up the mountain it started, but by its size at that point, it must have been several klicks.

Jim was the fourth member back, and when it was his time to drop into the water, he thought, *damn good thing we were not running. Hell, coming on this out of nowhere, the fall would have killed us.* As he dropped into the water on the slippery rocks, he lost his balance and landed on his butt, causing a splash and more noise than he would like. No one said a word. They just looked to see if he was okay. He held his left hand up with his thumb in the air, regained his footing, and then moved forward, allowing the man behind him to drop into the creek.

Moments later, a very eerie group of men dressed in green with war paint covering their faces, necks, and hands, with boonie hats draped on their heads, stretched out some five to seven meters apart, very slowly making their way down the creek.

The water's depth ran from calf-high to waist-high, and the width of the water itself was about three to five feet, with the creek bed running from a few feet wide to touching the steep banks. The water flowed over a rocky creek bottom, making it most difficult to walk in, and then it would drop into a pool of water that reached one's waist. Jim kept wondering when Hawk would go through one of the pools and just drop over his head. But they were in the upper parts of the creek, so that would most likely not happen until they got to the lower end of the creek if they got that far. He was hoping they would not have to travel that far down toward the valley floor.

The foliage would change from a complete overhead canopy, where even the sun at high noon made it rather dark. When the sunlight did penetrate through the heavy overhead canopy, it created streams of light rays filtering through the trees, making it look as if some heavenly host was about to appear in all its celestial glory before the group of men in single file wading down some blessed mountain waters. The trees positioned on the top edges of the creek banks had a multitude of large and medium side roots that extended openly through the sides of the steep banks and extended down into the creek bed.

Then, as if one were coming out of a cave, there would be an opening in the canopy, and the sky would be clear, and the hot sunlight would pour down onto the small patrol. The foliage on the sides of the creek bank would turn to the long, thick, green grasses that seemed to have a razor edge to them. Rusty would tell us, "It is as bad as the cord grass in Texas, cut you to shreds." These grasses were over six feet tall and so thick that one could not penetrate them without difficulty. The grasses' long blades would drape over the sides of the top of the bank, nearly reaching the creek bed itself. Hanging loosely and moving with the slightest breezes like long tentacles, they appear to be reaching out with their rough sandpaper surface attempting to gulp you into its hundreds of waving blades. The larger broadleaf plants were often mixed in with the grasses in and around the trees under the canopy.

After ninety minutes of slowly wading the creek, the patrol took a break as they again entered another darkened overhead canopy forest. The under-foliage in the dark shaded areas was different from the open spaces. Larger and broader plants covered the ground area. Each man alternated to each side of the creek placed themselves against the banks, blending into the roots of the trees that reached down into the edge of the water like giant legs that were attached to some towering giant forest creature.

Jim welcomed the cool, damp ground of the bank on the backs of his legs and buttocks. The creek bed area was only three feet from the water's edge. He leaned back against the side of the bank, which was only about six feet in height. He removed his boonie hat, then leaned forward and scooped up a hat full of water and poured it over his head, letting the cool water soak his upper body. He sat back into the roots, laying his head between them. His shaved, war-painted head and face made it almost impossible to be seen as he closed his eyes and listened for anything that was not normal to the forest into which they were descending deeper and deeper.

In the distance, he could hear the sharp howl of a monkey and the odd sound of some bird unknown to him. The sound of the rippling, briskly clean, clear water over the rocks as it flowed to the valley far below was soothing to his mind. But mostly, he heard silence, a welcome sound to his ears. As he sat, savoring the moments of silence, his thoughts went to the creek that descended into the river by the home he grew up in and the two mountains that towered high above the river. He thought of how, long before the Long Hunters penetrated the virgin forests of southwestern Virginia, and over time how the white man had polluted the streams, as well as the creek that cascaded over hundred-foot-high falls before it emptied into the river a quarter of a mile away. The creek had, over the eons, cut its path between the two mountains to empty into the river directly across from his home place. A creek he had explored from its mouth to its source a three-mile journey back up into the open area of a valley between yet more mountains to the south. He thought that at one time, long ago, it too must have been just as clean and clear. A time when the Native Americans were roaming the area, and to his knowledge, it was a pristine hunting ground for several tribes that filtered into the area to do their hunting.

Every inch of his clothing was wet with sweat or creek water. He was tired even before he had left for the mission. He wished he could relieve himself of the weight of personal supplies he was carrying, relax where he sat, and sleep for just a few hours, secure in knowing his concealment was secure from anyone who might happen by. He did not feel hungry, although it had been several hours since he had eaten, and whatever food he had consumed for breakfast had already been burned. There had been a minimal conversation between the patrol members as they sat and ate their breakfast. No one wanted to talk about the mission and where they were heading.

He knew that a power nap was not possible and that he would be up and moving again in a matter of minutes. The food would come late in the day. Sleep would not come at all. So he opened his canteen, took a small drink of water, replaced it on his side, closed his eyes, and just listened.

Another hour of walking the creek, trying not to fall on the slippery rocks and traversing between the large boulders where the stream gushed between them since they had started their descent in the pristine water, then suddenly a fist went up from the point man. Jim went down on his right knee into the water and pivoted slightly to his left, his AR-15 at the ready, quickly scanning the area in front of him. Hawk slowly worked his way back to the first Yard and whispered that he had spotted a major trail leading down into the creek on both sides of the bank. The word was passed back in the same manner.

As the patrol very alertly and slowly advanced to inspect the trail, they saw that it was well worn and was about four feet wide, very large for a trail through the jungle, which meant that it was a major roadway for the VC to haul their supplies. The bank on each side of the creek had been carved out, allowing easy access down into the creek. The patrol gathered and plotted the trail on their maps at the creek crossing, then cautiously proceeded up the left side of the trail. It ran between two ridges like fingers that ran to the creek from the top of the mountain. For Jim, a hollow was all it was. Jim found himself more alert. His heart began to pump faster, not because of the incline but because it was a trail that was worn smooth, which meant that many people traveled it. These people would not welcome the patrol with open arms if they met anywhere along the path.

The hollow twisted and turned gently upward for about a mile (two klicks) with only two branches that Jim could tell. Neither branch had any paths that intersected into the central hollow. As the patrol approached the top of the ridge, the trail led off to the west and along the ridgeline. The patrol traveled along the ridge for about 3.22 kilometers (two miles) and stopped. After a hand-and-whisper discussion, they backtracked to the creek and followed the trail up the other side of the mountain. The same topography was on the northwest side of the creek as was on the southeast side. However, the path to the southeast side of the ridge meandered along the mountainside instead of up any hollow. As a result, it took the patrol longer to reach the top of the ridge on the southeast side. Once at the top of the ridgeline, the trail followed along the spine, and according to their maps, the ridge's backbone descended to the valley like tributaries to a river. This meant that the traffic in the valley, which was already known, was coming from the Cripple Creek Patrol area. This was what they were looking for. For Jim, this meant that they were in great danger. He and the others realized that the odds were great that they would not get out of this mission without being compromised. Now, as the patrol sat at the top of the ridge, planning the best place to be for the night, what worried Jim was if they would get out at all.

His mind wandered briefly as the rest of the patrol talked in whispers and hand signals. He looked around and realized that the entire forest was a rather enchanting and mysterious place to be. It was so peaceful and filled with incredible beauty, and yet amid all the beauty he saw, he felt the darkness and horror of war and death, causing him to shake as his body suddenly felt chilled. He was quickly brought back into the reality of where he was. Hawk asked him where he thought they should set up for the night, in hopes that they would observe the traffic that they felt traveled the mountain path on a nightly basis, carrying the supplies of war.

Jim looked at Bill and then at Rusty. The long-distance look in his eyes must have told them everything, as his mind was yet streaking back to reality.

"You all right, Jim?" Rusty whispered.

"Yes," Jim whispered, then unfolded his laminated, covered topographic map, laying it out on the ground. Looking at it for a few seconds, Jim pointed his finger to a line he had drawn with his grease pencil. It denoted the trail leading up the hollow and out of the top of the ridge on the northwest side of the creek. He quickly drew a black line on the topographic map denoting the southeast side of the trail and extended it down to where the ridge ended in the valley.

"Here. I think we should recon this area here and set up for the night."

"Why there?" Hawk whispered.

"Because here," he said, pointing and tapping the map, "we can observe them coming down the hollow. So we will be on the upper side of "Charley," looking down into the hollow, and still see enough to get an idea of how many and how often and still be safe."

"Damn, that is awful thick shit over there," Rusty started in a whisper.

"Yeah, well, better not to be seen, my flat-landed Texas friend. Besides, on this side of the creek, it is too steep and too thick for us to get a good location to observe our little friends."

"We can recon the area during the day and observe during the night. That way, if we have to come back, we will have it plotted out for an ambush," Bill whispered, excited about the entire mission.

"Hawk made us not forget, this is their yard we are playing in, and they may very well travel during the day. But hell, they feel safe this deep in the jungle. They figure this trail will not be found. I mean, think about it—what are the odds that anyone would find this? Damn slim if you ask me. So, we can do some reconning, but we had better be damn careful. I mean, there ain't but six of us, and you know fuckin' well that there will be one hell of a lot more of them. The PZ is damn sure too far away to be running to. So getting anyone in here for a pickup is out of the question."

"Yeah, yeah, I got it. But if we were not good at what we do, we would not have found this trail to start with."

Jim just looked at Bill without saying a word. Rusty never said anything, as he knew that Jim went with his intuition, that little voice he always talked about, and most of the time, he was right. Two of the three Yards were off a few meters, one toward the valley side of the trail, the other the creek side. Y Jhon was kneeling on his left knee beside Rusty. He looked at O'Francis for a long moment, his dark eyes reading Jim's face as if he also felt the fear being revealed across his war-painted face.

Off they went back down the mountain, across the creek, and halfway up the mountain, where they reconned for the best sight to set up to observe for the next couple of days.

After finding the best place to see the trail, at a safe distance not to be seen, they settled in, spreading out along the side of the hill some six meters apart.

After removing his ninety pounds of gear and eating, Jim got comfortable intertwining himself into the foliage, becoming invisible. The mountain air was cooling, and he put on his field jacket. He closed his eyes and rested. His hearing increased tenfold for any sound that was not natural to the jungle. Darkness came rather quickly, or so it seemed. Jim looked at his illuminating watch. It was 2100 hours. He wondered if the traffic would come. But he did not have to wait all that long. By 2230 hours, he could hear the Viet Cong, and most likely North Vietnamese Regular Army, intermixed with the VC, coming from on top of the ridge. Jim thought, *they sure as hell are not quiet, but what the fuck—why should they be? They felt safe in their mountain sanctuary.* The length of soldiers and supply carriers stretched from the creek to somewhere on top of the ridge. Then there was a lull of about an hour or so, and another group traveled down the hollow.

Even though Jim could not be seen, his heart pounded so heavily that he could hear it in his ears as they went by. As the patrol waited, only two columns passed the first night. He could only estimate how many there had been, but the number was significant, and he knew it would take a major operation to pull off an ambush, if at all. As he lay and analyzed the possibilities, Jim concluded that there would be too many enemy forces for the A-242 and the Yards to conduct an ambush patrol from Dak Pek. In addition, they would be too deep into the jungle, and the terrain was too rugged for any large operation. One good thing about working with this group of soldiers, they would listen and take advice from the people who had done the reconnaissance of the area.

They reconned the entire area the next day, plotting every inch of the hollow from the creek to the top of the ridge. As they had to work at a snail's pace and as quiet as a slithering snake, it took them all day.

The next night, the same pattern occurred, almost at the same time. Jim logged the time in his head, as he was sure that Bill and Rusty had done the same. At 0600 hours, as the dawn was just breaking, giving them just enough light to move safely, they would backtrack up the creek and to the PZ. The sound of people was heard at the top of the ridge. At once, they were down again in silent watching mode. This time they could see more clearly between all the foliage. It took forty-five minutes from the first person Jim saw to the last person who passed in front of him. It appeared they were carrying everything from food supplies to weapons, including several large mortars, and several were pulling two-wheeled carts with supplies.

Jim's mind was racing; Christ, this is not good. Dear ole Charlie is preparing a major attack on someone. To ambush a patrol this size will take every yard we have. This is not good. Hell, I hate even telling SOG that we even found this fuckin' place. Jim's little voice kept talking to him as he lay and waited for over an hour after the VC patrol had passed.

Each one of the Cripple Creek Patrol slowly moved through the thick undergrowth along the hillside and over the top of a fingered ridge that formed the hollow—leading to the creek. They reached the creek within an hour of their descent. Jim estimated they were a good half mile up from where the main trail crossed the creek. He felt very uneasy as they made their way back up the creek. He wished they could have moved faster but knew they could not. He felt like a turtle trying to trek up the creek as his heart pounded with anxiety. He tried to calm himself, telling himself they would not run into rogue patrols this far from the trail. They had seen no signs of trails leading down from either side of the mountain as they had come down the creek. He recognized where they entered the creek as they pushed onward up the stream, looking for a better place to exit the area and make their way through the jungle and to the rendezvous, about four kilometers from where they had been let out three days earlier. He had no doubts that the ever-dependable "Green Taxi" would be at the coordinates on time. The question was, could they?

Another two miles up the creek, the bank on the west side feathered out enough for the Cripple Creek Patrol to easily exit the creek area and begin their snail's pace through the jungle, picking their way as quietly as possible. By the time they reached the top of the ridge, Jim was soaking wet, his legs ached, his back ached, he had a headache that was pounding like kettledrums, and he was not in a good mood. The humidity was so high that it was hard to breathe. There was no breeze. Jim surmised that the temperature was in the upper nineties. As they rested and plotted where they were from the maps, clouds began to move over the mountain, and in a matter of minutes, it was raining so hard that if one could have seen twenty yards in any direction, they couldn't. The rain felt good; it was a cool rain, and Jim welcomed it. He knew that just as soon as it was over—and it would stop just as quick as it had begun—the humidity would be just as bad if not worse if that were possible.

They made their way along the ridgeline up and down as it raised and lowered in the topography. Like some theme park roller-coaster ride, then, without any notice, they came upon a trail. Smaller in width, maybe two meters wide, but well used, they all stopped and located where they were on the maps, again plotting the trail. The patrol pulled back several yards off the trail. The trail appeared to lead in the same direction they had to travel. One of the Yards headed in the opposite direction where the patrol was traveling to see if he could determine where it may be going or coming from. He returned in ten minutes with a report that it dropped off the back side of the main ridge just a short way out the top of the ridge, maybe one kilometer at best.

"So, what do you think?" "Hawk," whispered.

"I say we take the fucking trail," Rusty stated. "I am fucking tired of trying to get through that shit and not make any fucking noise."

"Hawk" looked at Jim. O'Francis pulled his boonie-hat off, looked at the map, looked back at Rusty and then at Bill, then at Y Jhon. "Shit, I don't know. Sure would make it easier on us to get where we need to be."

Rusty whispered, "So, how do you feel? I mean, you know?"

Bill was talking to Y Jhon and the other two Yards and looking at the map. Jim had not responded for several seconds.

"Well?" Rusty asked again.

Jim looked at Rusty for several more seconds.

"Damn, Rus, I just don't like this fucking area. I don't know. I have had a bad feeling since I learned we had to recon this damn AOL."

"Ahh, hell, O'Francis, God damn it, one place is just as bad as another. It's all fucked up. You know that shit, man. Let's take the damn trail and just get the fuck out of here. Come on, what do you say?"

"Okay, hell, you are probably right. One place is just as bad as another—no telling what or when you will run upon a patrol. Shit, we can handle it. Right?" He and Rusty looked at each other.

"Right, by God! Fuck it! We are Rangers. We can handle it!"

Bill made his way back over to Jim and Rus. "So, what do you want to do?"

"Take the trail," Rusty stated. Jim just nodded.

"Okay." "Hawk" took the point once again, and they were off.

They had traveled an hour and were making good time. The patrol would be at the PZ a good half day at their current pace before they were to be picked up. The trail kept to the top of the ridges most of the time, dropping off to one side or the other for several meters from time to time. Then they were back on top of the ridgeline for several hundred yards, and then they began descending slowly straight down as the path, following the topography of the ridge into a gap between the ridgeline. They crossed over several large outcroppings and then another stretch of the relatively smooth trail where the jungle foliage touched them on both sides as they walked along.

All Jim heard was the sound of an AR-15 and then the resounding reply of the AK-47s. He saw Rusty dive to his right, and Jim went to his left into the thick foliage of the jungle. He heard Hawk yell that they were direct to his front. Jim and the Yard behind him moved quickly along the side of the path toward Bill, a matter of a few meters. Rusty and Y Jhon moved through the undergrowth on the opposite side. Seeing the enemy's location was difficult. The sounds were not. O'Francis and the Yard engaged about the same time Rusty and Y Jhon did. The advantage went to the Cripple Creek Patrol as they were on the upper side, and the movement of the Viet Cong allowed them a target to shoot at.

Jim yelled at Rusty that he and Y Bang were moving up to Hawk's position on the downslope side. As they did, he could see the line of fire and the movement of the VC trying to circle on Bill and Y Jhon's position. They opened fire instantly and saw a body fall. As they continued to lay down fire, he could hear Rusty engaging, and within a matter of minutes, there was once again silence. No sounds from the forest, no sounds of rain falling, nothing. Several minutes passed before O'Francis yelled for Rusty. He got a return. "Okay." Then he heard Rusty moving, and in seconds, he called out to Jim as quietly as possible that Hawk had been hit, Y Jhon was okay. Several more minutes passed before Y Bang and Jim moved toward Bill's position. They had not heard any movement from the ten to thirteen meters directly in front of them for several minutes after the firefight had stopped.

As Jim and Y Bang arrived at Bill's position, they found Rusty caring for a left-shoulder wound. Y Jhon was positioned just to his front on alert. Y Bang turned and moved a few meters to their rear and took up a position. They quickly patched the "Hawk-man" up, and he was on his knees, sitting back on his calves, his boonie hat draped on the back of his neck, supported by its string. He looked up at Rusty and then Jim.

"Damn, how close can that get? Shit. Hell, I barely saw them. Son of a bitch! What the hell!"

Jim smiled for the first time in three days. "Well, I am sure glad you saw them first, Mr. "Hawk." Jim gave Bill a nickname because of his nose and not his excellent eyesight, as his nose had a beak look to it from being broken several times. Of course, it was easy as his last name was Hawkins. However, Jim always liked giving people he liked nicknames.

"Hey, we are not far from the PZ. We should be there in a few hours. So I'll take the point. You drop back in front of Y Bang," Jim stated.

Y Jhon worked his way down to the VC patrol and checked the dead. As he returned, Bill was just getting to his feet.

"There were six, all dead."

"We need to get them off the trail a few meters before we go," Rusty stated.

After getting Mr. Charles and his Commie buddies off to both sides of the trail several meters, the Cripple Creek Patrol proceeded down the trail through the swag on the ridge and up the other side.

As Jim crested the top of the ridge, he could hear voices and movement coming up the trail. He figured the sound of the firefight would bring any other patrols to their location in a hurry. Quickly his arm went up. He turned and pointed to his ears and then pointed down toward where they were headed. Waving left and right, the CCP quickly disappeared into the jungle on either side of the small pathway. As he lay camouflaged into the jungle floor, he could hear the patrol quickly passing, almost in a run. He waited for several minutes, giving them plenty of time to reach the swag in the ridgeline, about three hundred meters away. Then, as if they all had some sixth sense, they moved in unison back onto the trail and proceeded to their PZ. They settled in and waited on their ride.

A clearing on top of one of the ridges was all they needed. Then, off in the distance came the sound of the deep throb of the "Green Taxi." Moments later, it was hovering on the small opening in the jungle at the top of the mountain ridge. As the last man of the Cripple Creek Patrol was on board, the green UH-1 Huey lifted just above the surrounding tree line and slanted eastward, gaining altitude with each passing second.

☿

The ducks brought Jim back to the world he now lived in. They had, for whatever reason, lifted off the water and turned and flown back over O'Francis' head in a flutter of wings and quacking. Jim looked at his watch. It was 1930 hours by his time, and he did not feel like fishing anymore, so he waded to the pasture side of the river and began his walk back to his truck.

Middle-School Experiment

As Bobby Simms had stated, "If you need anything ... " Jim went to him on the last working day of the teachers' workdays before the students arrived and questioned Mr. Simms about his qualifications to teach a sixth-grade class. His certification was for secondary, grades nine to twelve, and junior high, grades seven and eight. However, Simms got around that by telling him that he was qualified because they were departmentalized and certified in the subject matter. Jim did not debate the issue, as he knew Reynolds County bent all the rules to fit whatever they needed. He always did his best to remember the Mark Twain quote. He was well aware that no one in the upper ranks of the department of education in Richmond did any checking on such small, insignificant matters as teacher qualifications in any field.

James Patrick had seen too many "teachers" teaching in areas where they were not even qualified or certified. Reynolds County School System did not adhere to Virginia's teacher certification rules. It was who you knew or blew that mattered, not the education of the youths.

Of course, he also knew that was one of the significant reasons Reynolds County School System was twenty-five years behind the rest of the nation in education. They would never catch up with the current superintendent and his puppet school board. The members who sat on the board were not qualified for the lofty positions they held. It was based solely on whoever was politically connected and would move their mouths when the strings were pulled. Most of the time, the entire school board's collective IQ would not equal eighty, which reflected their actions and their method of thought toward education as a whole. Over the many years, school boards would change, but the lies, corruption, and stupidity were always the same.

The months of August, September, and October went about as Jim expected them to go, semi-smooth, with his new colleagues being distant, having little communication with him as if he had some plague. Jim was the last to be informed of anything going on regarding meetings or places he was to be or for his classes. The students kept him informed as to any changes in the schedule.

Jim, of course, arrived on more than one occasion a few minutes late to assemblies or programs that were suddenly changed, which made him look like he was uncooperative, causing some of the women teachers who outnumbered the men by twenty to one to gossip about him and his alleged reputation of being insubordinate to the administration. James Patrick was adjusting or trying to, as he had never taught a junior high class before, and his current students' age and mental capabilities were way below what he was accustomed to.

It was not easy for him to get to the level of sixth and seventh graders. He found that they were ill-prepared for a junior high school class setting. Of course, the freshman students he had taught for many years were ill-prepared for high school, making a bold statement about the quality of middle-school teaching. The students had been pampered and spoon-fed on a level below the grade they were. The grading system was the same as at the high school, antiquated. Giving the students high-level grades was not out of the norm to make the teacher look good in the administration's eyes and make parents happy. Jim just did not do that. He taught a level higher than what they were to bring them up, not down. He believed in making them think. They were not too young to think about questions presented to them verbally in his lectures or on a test. James Patrick did not waver in his teaching and testing style.

He continued to lecture, slowing down until the students got used to taking notes. He would teach them how to take notes in each individual's type of shorthand. There were no true-or-false tests, no fill-in-the-blanks, and no multiple choice, only short-answer questions, which had to be in complete sentences. After a short while, he would work on at least two short-essay questions. That would require thinking. He carried his classroom title of O'Francis' "Think Tank" to the middle school.

A few parents protested to the administration about their children taking notes and the type of tests. The administration brought the issues to the attention of James Patrick. He listened professionally and responded intellectually, giving sound reasons for his methods of teaching as well as testing. As Jim saw it, one of the major problems was that most parents in the area considered the sixth and seventh grades to be elementary. They had not grasped the middle school concept designed to prepare students for high school. The school system itself had not grasped either. The eighth grade was located at the high school and was part of high school in most uninformed minds. This concept gave the impression that "they" were in high school. In the minds of the students and parents of Reynolds County, you had two levels, elementary school, and high school.

He had always tried to prepare his students for the next-highest level of education. Now his work was cut out for him. He faced the same gossipy criticism from any number of his new colleagues in a building that housed kindergarten through seventh grade. The students advancing from their elementary environment into a middle-school environment were ill-prepared, especially when entering O'Francis' "Think Tank."

James Patrick hoped that the seven teachers located in the middle-school section of the school were different from those he had been dealing with for the past fifteen years at the high school level. He hoped they would be "real teachers," not just to collect another paycheck, padding their yearly family income with what their husbands or mates made. He was hoping that it did not look like rats scurrying to flee a burning building at three-thirty. The few he would be working with were the type who put forth the effort to be a good educator, which took many long hours outside their regular classroom daily. He hoped that what he had heard over the years was not correct— games and playtime, with little actual instruction taking place.

Over time, he would learn who the real educators were and who was there for the paycheck. It always showed in the students who entered his Think Tank, which reflected an inferior product for the next level of education. Jim realized why he had gotten so many students as freshmen and sophomores, who were not prepared. There were, of course, exceptions with his young students. Several students were standouts for their ages of twelve to thirteen years. Several would excel in O'Francis' Think Tank and go on to excel in high school as well as in college. Jim related a story about Josh Pickens, who obtained a Rhodes scholarship and a Ph.D. from the University of Virginia.

O'Francis reminded me of a conversation he had when he first arrived in Honsburg. The insulting discussion with one of his colleagues concerning the students' learning skills in the Appalachian Mountains. He told me he hated it then, and he hated it during our conversation. Jim had a simple philosophy. A person who carried the title of a teacher had an enormous responsibility—opening up the minds of the youths and inciting knowledge. It did not matter if it was in the inner city or the Appalachian Mountains. The student would learn if the teacher would make it presentable in a manner that made them thirsty for more knowledge and not bore them to the point that they shut down the learning center, the brain.

Shortly after his first year at the middle-school level, he discovered that one of his students did not fit the age group. *Young* was a significant understatement when O'Francis found that Noble Bryan was only ten years old. Jim had difficulty understanding how a ten-year-old was in his sixth-grade world geography class. However, he soon learned that he was a child prodigy, a reticent, excellent student. Jim would have the young Noble for two straight years and enjoyed his learning skills. His sponge-like brain absorbed every ounce of knowledge that Jim put out. James Patrick could not see the future, but in time, he would run across the man named Nobel, who became a computer genius and worked for none other than the unappreciative Reynolds County School System.

The typical Reynolds County School Board was ignorant about the technological world growing exponentially right before them. The school board members had no interest in learning about such a world because of their lack of education, yet they sat at the head of a school system, putting on the façade of being important. Jim once stated in one of our more intense discussions concerning the intellectual level of the elected school board members, "Twain" said it best; "Never argue with ignorance. They will drag you down to their level and then beat you with experience."

That was why Jim did not attend many school board meetings. He could not stand to be in the presence of so many stupid people playing demigods. Of course, as O'Francis often would state, in our lengthy conversations about the school system, "You just cannot fix stupid!"

Another one of Jim's students appeared on the scene on a warm August morning, Bruce Vidal. However, I am getting ahead of my story, the tech department staff, and their relationship with J. Patrick O'Francis. I will pick up this part of his story later on in the ever-challenging world of Jim O'Francis.

Happy Anniversary

In late September, J. Patrick went squirrel hunting, something he had not done in many years. He enjoyed that type of hunting; no real danger in some overzealous hunter shooting him. He had been asked to go deer hunting on several occasions by several people, but he could not bring himself to gamble on that kind of hunting. He told me a story about his acquaintance, a Viet Nam Veteran who went deer hunting and was killed. He was covered in bright orange from head to toe. Shooting a deer for Jim was not the problem. He enjoyed eating venison, lean meat, and very little fat. The point of fact was, it was his favorite meat, as long as someone else made the kill and just brought it to him to clean and cut up.

Shooting a rodent was a world of difference for Jim; besides, he did not like rodents of any kind. He got great pleasure in hunting them down and killing them. Of course, he enjoyed eating the squirrels, but the game he played hunting them was the most fun. It was the challenge of moving ever so slowly through the forest with only the sounds of nature surrounding him. Hiding and sneaking up on them and then getting them in his sights with his .22-caliber single-shot rifle. He always used his old single-shot he had gotten when he was thirteen years old. He earned money for his first gun by being a caddy at the local golf course, and his grandfather helped him buy it. He had several shotguns, more modern, more shots, but it was the challenge again, one shot, one squeak, that he enjoyed.

Fall was in full color the last week of October and the anniversary of James Patrick and Dawn Christine O'Francis. Their day had been carefully planned and mapped out as they stopped by the corner gas station to fill their car up with fuel. It was a little after nine in the morning, and the October mountain air was crisp as Jim stood at the gas pump. He wore a lightweight tan jacket, jeans, and soft-sole high-top hiking shoes. Dawn sat behind the car's steering wheel, windows up, and the heater on light warm to offset the chill. He did not see who was in the car that had pulled in beside the pumps at the island to the far side of the service station lot. He finished filling his car, placed the nozzle back into the pump holder, opened the door, and told Dawn how much the cost was. She wrote a check; in a small town, one could do so if one was known to have good credit. He picked up some two-day-old newspapers and an empty paper coffee cup to be placed in the trash can to the rear of the island. Then, taking the check and closing the door, he turned and walked toward the closed double-glass doors of the cash-and-carry store.

"I didn't know they let assholes like you out this early in the morning!"

Jim stopped and turned as he recognized the voice of Richard Finkel. He thought, *Ahhh, hell, he is not worth ruining my day. Fuck him!*

Turning away, he went in to pay for his gas. Mary Jo Bankos was the cashier that morning. She was talking to Gerry Bare, who was getting a cup of coffee at the counter's far end.

"Good morning, Coach, how are you today?" Mary asked with a warm tone and a smile on her face.

"Morning, Mary," Then he looked toward Gerry. "Top O' the morning to you, Gerry."

"Morning, Jim. Good to see you again."

"You too, Gerry, but I believe I would find a better person to ride with than the piece of shit you are riding with today!"

Gerry had a little laugh, and still smiling, said, "Well, gotta get a ride with whomever; no choice in the matter today."

Jim turned and walked toward the double glass doors, waving back over his shoulder. "See ya, Mary Jo, see ya, Gerry." Then he exited the store. As James Patrick walked toward his car, Finkel was walking toward the store doors.

"Got rid of your ass, didn't I!" Richard stated as he pointed his finger at Jim, walking in his usual cocky, strutting manner.

Enough was enough. Jim turned from the direction of his car and walked toward Finkel.

"You have shot off the mouth lots as of late, Richard." Jim's tone was cold and hard.

They had walked within three feet of each other. James Patrick pulled off his marrow-style sunglasses and dropped them on the concrete paving to his left.

"Now, Finkel, we are not on your protected school grounds, and you have stated to several people in this community how you were going to kick my ass if you ever caught me out in public. So, here I am! Do you still want that piece of ass? If so, then let's you and I do a little dancing!"

Finkel froze. His eyes widened, his hands began to tremble, and he lowered his head, looking at the concrete at his feet.

"No," he replied in a much lower voice. His entire demeanor changed from only moments earlier. He had not figured in the fact that Jim would ever confront him with witnesses only a matter of fifty feet away inside the store. He had also calculated Gerry was coming to his aid if Jim started anything. Unfortunately, he had miscalculated on all counts.

"What? I do not think I heard you, Richard! Now is the time to back up that big mouth of yours. I mean, you made the statements to several people, so let's dance. You get to take that big shot you've been bragging about!"

Inside the store, Mary and Gerry looked out the door at the two men and looked at each other. Neither spoke. Gerry simply shrugged his shoulders, smiled, and took a drink of coffee, then stated," I damn sure am not going to challenge O'Francis. We have no beef with each other."

Jim took a step toward Richard, coming within an extended arm's length of Richard Finkel.

"No," he replied again in a meek tone, not the arrogant, cocky tone and posture he usually displayed. Jim was calm, his feet slightly apart, with his right foot just to the rear of his left, his body turned ever so slightly to his right, his arms to his side, his left thumb tightly wrapped over his fingers, forming a fist, his right flattened and stiffened and pointing downward. There was no doubt he meant business and was baiting Finkel to find enough man in him to strike him. Jim locked his vacuous eyes on Richard's downward look; a slight breeze began to blow the cool thirty-five-degree air around the corner of the building.

"Well, Mr. "*badass*," here I am. I am waiting for my *ass-kicking*! What do you say? Do we get it on here so you can tell all your asshole political buddies how you kicked old Jim O'Francis' ass all over the street or not?"

Richard had not looked up from the concrete and once again stated, "No."

"Well, since we ain't going to dance, then I am telling you here and now, mister, you keep your fucking mouth shut about how you are going to kick *my ass*, and as for you *getting rid of me*, you and your other pieces of shit have made a horrible mistake! You people have fucked with the wrong self-made son of a bitch this time! My time *will* come! You can bet on that one. 'Mr. Bookie,' put a lot of money down on it, because it will take place! My time, my place!"

James Patrick stepped back one long step, squatted down, never taking his eyes off Richard, picked his sunglasses up, placed them to his eyes, pivoted sharply, and calmly walked to the car. Dawn did not know what had happened, as she had been grooving to the oldies on the radio. With that, Jim and Dawn drove off. After hiking and spending time in the forest, the two ended their day that evening with a bottle of fine wine and very well-prepared food at a nice steakhouse.

Damon, Finkel, Duncan, and Marshy gathered in Marshy's office for the plan to put O'Francis out of the teaching business for good. Damon would write a letter to Marshy claiming that O'Francis confronted

Finkel while on assignment for the school, threatening his life and Finkel's. He would include in this letter that Mr. O'Francis had in the past threatened Damon's life with terrorist acts, as well as several other teachers in the school. Damon would claim that O'Francis had conducted terrorist acts toward several other community members and that they had personally requested that he do something about O'Francis. Damon would include in the letter that he and Finkel feared for their life and property. He would ask that the school board remove him from the school system as a teacher. In his letter to the school board, he stated that type of person should not be allowed around children. He, as well as many parents, considered him unstable and unfit to teach. He would include in the letter that, at present, he feared for the safety of several of his teachers and several parents and their children because of personal threats made by O'Francis to parents and children.

It was conceived that day that Damon would send a copy of this letter to their good political friend Judge Edwin, all the local law-enforcement departments throughout the area, and the state police.

A copy of the letter was to be sent especially to their ally, Trooper Penrod.

"I think we should also send a copy to the FBI," Damon said with evil glee. No response to Damon's statement among the men in LaMar's office.

LaMar was the first to respond to Damon's suggestion. "I don't know about that. I mean...well, we are okay within our area. Hell, we all know that. But shit, the FBI? Hell, I don't think we should go there."

Damon insisted. "Why not? I mean, it really would be the doom for the son of a bitch!"

"Yeah, well, Damon, it damn well could be the doom for all of us when you get the FBI involved in this. Hell, do you have anybody in the FBI that can pull any weight for us?" Duncan spoke for the first time in the meeting.

At the moment, among the power structure of the school system, Finkel wanted to show his strong support for his principal. Thinking it would give him some importance. "I think we should. I think it is a safe bet."

More silence as Marshy was up pacing across his large office. First, he would look at Duncan to get a political read from the leading board of supervisors.

Then, finally, a very slight movement of the head, indicating a no, and Marshy spoke.

"Look, let's not bring in the federal people. We have no control over them at all. We do not want to get in over our heads here. I mean, we can handle this little matter in our backyard. Hell, he is just a fuckin' teacher, a small pimple on our ass. But, shit, Damon, sometimes you get too goddamn carried away."

Using several colorful metaphors, Damon Bales exploded and concluded with, "I want him gone!"

"Look, Damon, lower your voice," LaMar came back in a harsh tone. "You have forgotten just who is in charge here. I make the final decision here, so just calm down." LaMar walked to his desk, sat down, and looked at all three men present in the office.

"Okay, we send the letter to all area law-enforcement people. Except for the FBI! Now Damon, make it happen."

He rose, and the meeting was over. Damon would do it his way. He was obsessed with the destruction of James Patrick O'Francis.

It was early December and time for O'Francis to renew his special police license, as William Peng had advised him after the Democratic Party had elected a new sheriff, one that they could control. Jim had done so and had kept them up to date for the past six years. Jim earned extra money as security in a local mall. In addition, he would, from time to time, help honorable police officers in the area who had been loyal democrats and had been given jobs as county deputies. Some were his former students.

He arrived at the courthouse at 1000 hours to meet with Judge Edwin. Jim informed the secretary that he had an appointment with the judge, and in a moment, the "good" judge came out of his office.

"Come in, Mr. O'Francis." Jim walked into his office.

"What can I do for you today?"

"Your Honor, I am here to get my special police license renewed for the twenty-ninth district."

He paused and then went to the far corner of his office where several file cabinets were, opening the second drawer down from the top of one of the cabinets. He pulled out a file folder, withdrew a sheet of paper, turned and walked to the corner of a large wooden, glossy-topped rectangular table, and placed a letter in front of James Patrick. "Have you seen this?"

Jim looked down at the paper and asked if he may look, and the judge acknowledged him. Then, taking a minute or so to read the letter, he looked up at the judge, stating in total surprise, "This is a joke, correct?"

"I don't think so, or I don't take it as a joke."

"Well, Your Honor, this is just an out-and-out lie! I mean, you don't believe all this, do you?"

Judge Edwin picked up the letter and looked at it. "Mr. O'Francis, I cannot see me having someone like you working for my court!"

Jim protested quickly. "Your Honor, these statements are false! Lies! This is clearly slander! I have had an impeccable record working for the police department. I have assisted in many cases and never, not once ever been reprimanded. On the contrary, I have adhered to the law, by the book."

"I am refusing to give you a special police license," he said as he held the letter toward O'Francis.

"I see ... well ... then I would like a copy of this letter, Your Honor." He paused for a moment and then walked to his door, which was never closed.

"Ann, would you make a copy of this for me?" He stood at the door while his secretary made a copy of the letter, walked to where Jim was still standing and gave him the document. "Have a good day, Mr. O'Francis."

Jim turned and did not respond, walked out of his office, and went straight to Dan's office. The refusal to give Jim a renewal of his special police license would mean that he could not work private security nights and weekends, which he was doing to offset the loss of income incurred by his coaching duties.

Dan directed Jim to the office of Fitzroy, Philps, and Starnoc. All three attorneys read the letter and made several unflattering comments concerning the author of the letter and his connection to the superintendent.

One of the attorneys, Channy "Bob" Philps, came over to James Patrick, sitting in a chair at the corner of an office desk, and began touching his shoulder. Jim looked at him to say, *what the hell are you doing?* And Channy stated, "I just wanted to touch a terrorist. I have never been this close to one.

One thing that bothers me, you are a little light-skinned to be what is stereotyped as a typical terrorist."

At that, laughter erupted, but not to have Channy have all the fun of what Jim considered to be a grave matter, Kelly Fitzroy quickly stated, "He is Irish, part of the IRA, that type of terrorist."

Following more laughter from all three attorneys, only a slight smile crossed O'Francis' face. Then, with coldness in his voice that stopped the laughing as if someone had turned off the radio and only the sounds of silence could be heard, he said, "I think these people have underestimated me. I know they do not know me. I want to do this by the legal system if at all possible. I have no intentions of losing, one way or the other. Kelly, if I were you, I would not make too lightly of ole James Patrick's connections. You just may not be too far off! But you can be assured that the statements in this letter are bogus!"

As he held the letter up, with that statement, it was recommended by the association's lawyers that Jim file a lawsuit against Bales and Finkel for slander and defamation of character. When he left the attorneys' office and walked to his car, it was dark. Then, a little voice began talking to him.

Why did not one of the three men in the room offer to take the case? Was it because they would have to file it in Reynolds County, or was he not yet aware of other reasons? Most likely, the logic would be political. But it did not matter; he would play this game out to the end, and if he could not be vindicated of the wrong that had been splattered on him like mud and dirty water from a passing car on a country road on a rainy day, then he would in due time get his justice.

☿

Jim had tried diligently to get an attorney to take his case of slander and defamation in 1988, and he had gone all over southwestern Virginia. Each attorney would state that what had been done was wrong, both morally and most definitely ethnically wrong. However, all seemed to think that there was just not enough to win a lawsuit or, as Jim began to feel after the tenth trip to an attorney's office, that the entire area was a den of snakes all slithering and sliding over and around each other. Of course, according to their standards and policies, the teachers' association would not come to the aid of one of their own because his job was not being threatened, and even with his current slandering letter, they still would not come to his aid.

Jim always felt that the policy was another political scapegoat for the policymakers in Richmond. It reminded Jim of the Vietnam policy the Washington "assholes" had, *"You only shoot when you are shot at!"* If it just so happens you get hit while waiting, and if it was the shot that you did not hear, sending you home in a draped Star-Spangled Banner black rectangle box, "Oh, we are very sorry about the loss of your son, and all the other meaningless rehearsed bullshit words they verbalized for the grieving parents and wives. *Brilliant minds running this country and state*, he thought.

Dan found an attorney to take the case, which turned out not to be so easy. It was, after all, Reynolds County and had a very venal reputation.

It was Christmas 1989, and Jim was not at all happy. His son Michael was in his first semester of college, and Patrick was in Jim's seventh-grade history class. The vile powers within the school system had cost Jim and his wife ten thousand dollars in yearly income in one malicious stroke of the pen. Jim had no money to give his son for expenses and had taken away anything extra for Christmas. All they could do was keep the bills paid and their credit good, which left zero money to spend on anything of leisure. The Christmas gifts were on credit, and food was on credit, thanks to a very kind and giving grocery store owned by David Hart, whom Jim and Dawn would ever be indebted to and would never forget. There were months that they would even have to borrow money for the gas to be put in his car to get to work. All were hoping they could find a way to juggle the only pay they had coming into the house.

Dawn had been unable to get another job in the community, not that there had not been several jobs that had come open in places like the local bank, which they did business with, but she was never given a chance. No family ties in the community, political connections, or the most important, favors done for certain people. She could not go out of town to get a job; they had one car, now being used to take Jim back and forth to his workplace. All that had happened to the O'Francis family was not done by accident, nor did just a few individuals do it. It had been well planned and coordinated by a long list of people, with many in the wings helping to make even the little things go the way they wanted and why, and all because he would not come in line. He would not give up the principles that he lived. More important to his adversaries, he always seemed to know too much.

Jim's career was on its last link. He had sent out several applications to several surrounding counties, and he was patient with hopes. He had learned that attribute while on many recon missions where he would have to "lay-dog" for days at a time waiting for the quarry. He knew sometimes it took a while to get any response from school systems. Nevertheless, he felt that he would get some word from one of the counties about an upcoming job on the high school level and even a coaching opportunity along with the teaching. He was always a positive thinker and believed in himself, and what he could contribute to the well-being of the youths he was privileged to have in his classroom.

Many weeks passed and then months. Finally, Jim's little voice told him to make some phone calls to some of the old friends who dated back to his childhood, now in administrative positions within several schools' systems. He felt they would tell him straight up, and that was all he ever asked of anyone. What he learned sent James Patrick deeper into his dark world and awakened the side of himself that he feared. He once really liked that side of himself, the cold, callous, insensitive person that kept him alive in a life-and-death game. But now, a beautiful wife and two sons he adored above everything placed enormous stress on his mental status.

Three of the four old-time acquaintances informed Jim of the recommendations coming out of Reynolds County, from the central office to principals and athletic directors. His career had been torpedoed. He now was blackballed, according to the information he received. No one wanted to touch him. He was a bad apple and was on his last leg. He was trapped inside a system that smelled of a vile stench that would have gagged a fresh maggot. The powers in control were intent on seeing him fired as a teacher. They had destroyed him as a coach. Now all they needed was enough evidence to fire him as a teacher. His enemies felt like they had his gonads in a vise and needed the right combination of parents and principal to end it all.

He could not escape anywhere, not even to another state. The Central Office controlled what was sent to wherever. James Patrick's sources got him details of what was in his files. After reading them, he would not have hired himself, based on what he read. "My God, where are they getting this shit? Hell, they have taken insignificant events and skewed them to an incomprehensible point. Damn, these statements are just lies!" He went from verbally talking to himself to thinking.

The Unknown Connection

The phone rang twice, and it was answered in the middle of the third ring. "Hello?"

"Good morning, Maria."

"Morning, Daddy."

"Has Joseph left yet?"

"No, would you like to talk to him?"

"Yes, please. You have a good day, my dear."

"Thanks, Daddy, I will, and you too. I love you. Here's Joseph."

"Yes, sir," Joseph said.

"Joseph, Michael will be by to pick you up at eight."

"Yes, sir." The phone clicked silent. Joseph informed his wife, Maria, that he would not be using his car that her dad had sent Michael to get him. It was unusual for the "don" to send someone to get Joseph. Instead, he usually requested for him to come by his office.

Michael pulled in the black four-door BMW in the arched driveway on time, and by 8:05, they were on the way to Don Vincent Spadalini's home. He came from a rural Sicilian, rather large farming family to the United States to have a better life in 1960. He worked very hard, attended DePaul University, obtained a degree in accounting and business, and became a successful multimillionaire in the shipping and restaurant business. His connection with the Syndicate came through his business and his uncle, who passed away in 1983 at eighty-five, some fifteen years earlier. The Spadalini family was powerful and had connections worldwide.

Joseph had married Don Spadalini's only daughter and had entered the family on the ground floor, required to earn his way up the ranking order of the chain of command that existed within the family. It was Don Spadalini's way. You must work for what you get, no free rides, and no give-me because of who you are, who you marry, or who you know. Don Spadalini was a very stern man, all business, and very candid. He required a lot from his people, but he was more than fair with them, both monetarily and in benefits. He most definitely was a man of his word, and anyone who knew of him or was even remotely connected to him knew it.

Joseph gently knocked on the dark double oak den doors. "Come in, Joseph." He opened the door into a large thirty-by-thirty-foot room filled with books on shelves on two walls from the floor to the twelve-foot ceiling. There were several paintings by Remington of the Old West on the walls, a twenty-foot glass section on the far wall as you entered the den. In the middle of the glass wall was one glass door leading onto a large wooden cedar deck and beyond the deck a large, very private yard. Don Spadalini's office desk was centered in the middle of the room, with a phone and several folders on it in neat order off to his left. He had a cup of coffee in front of him and a large ashtray for his cigars. As Joseph entered, he was lighting his first-morning cigar, a Montecristo, seven inches long and known in the cigar world as a fifty ring. His phone rang as Joseph closed the door behind him. He took a seat in the dark-brown, deeply padded leatherback, soft pillow-top arms, and T-cushion chair, the only other chair in the room directly to the front of the desk. Vincent took several more puffs of his cigar and answered the phone. The conversation was short and direct, and then he placed the phone on its cradle.

"Joseph, I have several items I want some answers to." He reached to his left and placed one of the folders in front of him, opening it.

"I have been informed you have been busy with some out-of-state activity. However, I was unaware of any job arranged out of state. Now, do you want to let me in on what is going on?"

Just as Joseph started to speak, a peck came on the door, and it opened. The maid stepped in. "Don Spadalini, would you like for me to bring the coffee tray in?"

"Yes, please, and bring some Danish also, Teresa."

Teresa Piero worked for the Spadalini family for the past twenty years. Sophia, the wife of Vincent, had hired her. Sophia had known Teresa's family in the old country and had been requested to help Teresa out by bringing her to the United States and giving her a job. In addition, Sophia had made sure she had gotten an education while she worked for the family. Teresa turned and closed the door.

"Now Joseph, what is going on, and why did I not know about this?"

Joseph had been in the Spadalini family for twenty-five years and was very close to his father-in-law. Still, he also knew that his father-in-law was the head of a much larger family and that to do any type of business in the "Family," you went through the Don first. Joseph had worked his way up the ladder and had been given a large part of the business to run, with the oversight of his father-in-law. He began telling Don Spadalini what he had ordered and why, which took a good hour to explain it all and who was involved, and how Joseph had gotten involved. He informed Vincent of his ordeal with O'Francis and how they had become acquainted.

The conversation was only briefly interrupted when Teresa brought in the coffee tray and the Danish rolls. Vincent rarely got angry and listened intently to Joseph. He had a lot of questions concerning the people and the whole picture. Each action could lead back to the family, which was taken very seriously. Each activity had to be calculated down to the very micro-degree.

"Where is this friend of yours now?" Vincent asked.

Joseph paused. "I really am not sure. He left the area he was living some years ago without leaving word with anyone."

Another pause as Don Spadalini looked across at Joseph. "Okay ... make some inquiries and find him."

Joseph reassured his father-in-law that James Patrick was okay and unaware of his actions.

Don Spadalini relit his cigar. "I must go to the downtown office this afternoon. I want something by Friday."

Another pause as he rose from his chair, walked to the full glass windows and looked out over the back part of his estate. Then, without turning around, he asked, "Do you think this ... O'Francis, is that correct?"

"Yes, sir, that is correct."

"Do you think he would have approved of your action?"

"Well ..." Joseph rose and walked to the window to stand by Don Spadalini. "I am not really sure. I know his Irish background, and I know how he feels, and I know he knows what the cost is, and as he would phrase it, how 'the game' is played."

"Game, what do you mean, game?"

"For Jim and his military background, the action that is required and has taken place is considered a game."

"What was he in the military?"

"He was a Ranger/Special Forces that served two tours in Vietnam."

"Hmmm, I see." A few moments of silence as the two stood looking out the window. "What was he specialized in?"

"I don't know. Jim won't talk about it. I don't believe he would even talk to his wife. I am not sure about that, but I would bet he has never talked to anyone outside his home about it. I have been informed that he did not trust many people, if any."

"How far can he be trusted?"

"Well, sir, from experience and from our source in that part of the country, he is a man of his word. If he tells you something, he will hold to it, no matter what the cost."

"Are you sure?"

"Yes, sir, one hundred percent sure."

"Let's find out where he is, and then I will talk to you about the other matters later. Do nothing without my approval, Joseph. Do not act on your own again on such a matter. I know you meant well, and I understand you owe him a few favors. But do not act on your own again when it involves this family, *Capisci?*" Then he turned and looked his son-in-law in the eyes.

"*Capisco,* Don Spadalini."

Vincent Spadalini smiled and placed his hands on Joseph's shoulders. "You have done very well, and I know I do not tell you that enough. But now, I have work to do, and so do you."

They turned and walked to the den doors, with Don Spadalini's left arm across the back of Joseph's shoulders.

"How old is this, O'Francis?"

"Ahhh, I am not for sure, a few years older than I am. Maybe about sixty, but not sure. I do not think he is older than that. Let me think, I was twenty when he and I got acquainted, and he had already been in and out of the service, so, I think maybe he was twenty-five at the time, so that would make him, ahhh yep, about sixty, Vincent."

Deer Hunting

The father of one of O'Francis' students called and asked if he would like to have some deer meat but would have to do the cleaning and the cutting. He and his sons killed more than they could use and had thought of him. Given that it was his favorite kind of meat, he accepted and felt that Mr. Earl Millstone knew he had some financial problems and could use the meat. A few good people in and around the little town at the foot of the mountain were just good, honest, hardworking people. They did not control the political machine, nor did the political machine give a damn about them, except at election time. Then and only then did they even address any "little" people, the working-class people's concerns or problems.

It was "game" time again, and Rusty and Jim got to work together with four Yards on this mission. The briefing was held in the predawn hour, which was standard, and the SOG personnel provided the area map provided by the CIA, which the air force supplied with their aerial reconnaissance. According to some of the more flamboyant pilots, "the big eye in the sky" can snap a picture of two red ants fucking on a green leaf floating down the Dak Poko River. So the recon team should never question their work of art.

The team loaded onto their "green limousine" (the one with the plush interior and the bar in the back seat,) and they were off by 0500 hours. They crossed a very long and high mountain range in a very short time. According to the Huey boys of the army escort service, it was over 5,300 feet in altitude, and they did not reference high or low. It was in altitudes. Then suddenly, they dropped to the foothills and the valleys below, sending all of Jim's innermost organs up into his throat. He knew they did it on purpose and without any warning, knowing they enjoyed what they were doing and laughing to themselves at the very moment. Jim and the Huey pilots got along very well. He enjoyed their humor sometimes. They seemed to make him laugh just when he needed it. They were as good at their job as he was his, which for O'Francis meant they were the best, and that their "game" was just as dangerous as his, if not more so, as they were exposed to incoming rounds often. For damn sure, they put themselves in harm's way when they extracted a recon team out of a hot PZ in the middle of some jungle-laden valley.

They zagged east and west through the foothills and lower valleys of the mountain ridge they had just crossed. This action went on for a good five minutes. Then they put the brakes on as they announced that they had arrived at their predetermined coordinates on time and in one piece. And that they hoped that James Patrick and company had enjoyed their trip. They would return in four days to pick them up. They hoped they had a lovely, relaxing time watching the area's animal life. More humor Jim thought as the chopper came to a stop some six feet off the ground, and in no more than a beat of one of its blades, they were out, and the green limo was out of sight. The team was once again alone in the silence of the forest.

The temperature was in the mid-nineties by the time they started toward their observation point. The ridge ran in a multitude of double-humpback camel contours. According to their map, they needed to follow the ridge facing them and travel some five kilometers to a point where heavy traffic was taking place via intelligence reports. So now they had to verify all this before the super flyboys dropped a shitload of five hundred-and one thousand-pound firecrackers on the area. *Like they really gave a big rat's ass,* Jim thought. He may look like a fool with his baby face and shaved head, *but if the big eye in the sky could do all they said it could, why in the hell did they need him and his team to verify a damn thing? Damn, "Spooks!"*

It was midmorning before they arrived at their prescribed coordinates, a pinnacle of a ridge extending down sharply to the east. The ridge itself had been formed into a jagged knife-edge of outcroppings. Now it was up to Sergeant O'Francis to find an area where they could observe the hollow below. Jim's team reconned the entire area as quickly as possible, establishing a position fifty meters from the main trail. Then two kilometers toward the valley. However, they found that Mother Nature had provided an area some thirty meters long, about twenty-five meters down from the endpoint of the ridge, as the best location for their observation. From that point, they could see with their binoculars through a few openings in the forest to the valley some 150 meters away.

From what they could tell, two significant trails appeared to be entering the narrow valley and leading toward the river. *Close enough*, Jim told himself. O'Francis and Rusty knew that the traffic would most likely be heavy. However, giving the SOG officer his due, he had described it damn close in the briefing. But O'Francis knew that he did not know the difference between a hollow—or holler, as it would be pronounced in the mountains of southwestern Virginia—and a valley. For that matter, the difference between a hill and a mountain was damn sure different, *but hell*, O'Francis thought, *he probably came from the flatlands of the United States, where a rolling hill was a mountain, then went to West Point, so what the hell could he expect.*

There was little time for the four-person team to set themselves up for their waiting game. O'Francis thought it must be like deer hunting for the people in the mountain region where he grew up, where the hunter found a good spot to wait for the deer they wanted to come strolling along. Then bang, meat for the family.

The men and boys position themselves to wait for the deer to come by on the trail they usually used daily. Only on this hunt, were they to bag no game, watch and record, and afterward slip silently back to the predetermined PZ. But as one would expect, very rarely did any mission ever go as planned, and this one would turn out to be no different. For two and a half days, they "laid dog" and observed enough traffic that one would think that these people were going and coming to work daily. Like one would see on any New York street. Jim was not surprised at the amount of war supplies being physically moved down the hollow and across the ridge, then to the next hollow and down to the tributary that led to the larger river valley.

Obtaining all the information they were asked to get, the team began working back through the double humpbacks to be extracted. At the same time, a nonchalant V.C. patrol was working its way in the direction O'Francis' team had come two days earlier. Both patrols were working their way up the same hump and met at its top. The results were as expected. O'Francis' team got the edge, as the V.C. patrol had no clue that anyone else was in the area and talked among themselves casually. All ten Victor Charlies paid the ultimate price for being in the wrong place at the wrong time. Sergeant O'Francis' team suffered no losses or wounded. They laid the soldiers out alongside the trail side by side in an orderly manner. One, so they could be found, leaving a message about who had been in "their" backyard. He took his one trophy he was sure of, yet another message, and was very much aware they knew that the same person had been in another part of their "backyard."

Two, James Patrick knew they would be missed, and their comrades would come looking for them. He knew they too had families, and they too needed to know what had happened to them, or so he felt. Some of the Yards did not understand why O'Francis would do what he did. Rusty did and knew the "Yards" did not know that he had a great deal of respect for their skill and tenacity for "the game" they played.

Too often, the Special Ops teams had to try to locate a downed pilot, some with success, and some came up empty, which left the question, were they MIA, or were they KIA? So often, the families would never know and wonder what happened to their loved ones in the depths of their subconscious, never really closing the book on the events that would change their lives forever. He had learned that their ideologies were different, however. They were human, and he felt he was doing right by them—a caring spot in his usual hard-shelled exterior persona.

I had asked Jim once after he told me of his ordeal and after some time had passed. I went back to the events. "Why did you lay them out like that?" His answer was slow in coming, and he told me that he would like to think that people worldwide have the same personal feeling about their loved ones. I mean, it is a game. "I know it is a very deadly game, but we, the elite soldiers, had to play it and have played it from ever how long back in time. At the time, on that day, it felt just."

I laid that away in the recesses of my mind for future thought and maybe a conversation with him, as I still had many questions about his war experiences. However, I also knew that getting him to talk about Vietnam was rare, and I needed to tread lightly on the matter. So I did not ask but suspected that he did not speak to just anyone about his Vietnam experiences. So now one would have to ask, why me? I do not know.

The Legal Process Begins

Dan informed James Patrick that he had made arrangements to meet with an attorney in nearby Abetton, and he was to be there at 1600 hours on Tuesday. As he made the forty-five-minute trip, his mind became more and more stressed. How often had he presented his case to attorneys, and how often had they sat and just insulted him by pretending to be listening? One even nodded off to sleep as Jim looked up and stopped in the middle of a sentence. The attorney never even noticed. Jim stood and was walking out of the office before he snapped awake.

This new attorney was the first female attorney he had met over the years, and her office was in the upper part of the law office building, which had been a sizeable antebellum home. It looked like it would date back to the late 1800s or early 1900s. It was a large room, thirty feet by forty feet, with two windows, one to the back of her desk, some ten feet away, and the other window six feet to the left of one of two chairs located in front of her desk. The walls were old-style wood paneling, medium brown. The floor was wood with a rug covering the middle sections where the two chairs and the desk were set. To the back of the room was a long table with many files. Some boxes were on the floor in front of the table with files. A computer was at the left of her desk against the wall.

She rose from her desk as the secretary announced, "Ms. Donatello, this is Mr. O'Francis."

She walked toward Jim with her right arm extended out open-handed. "Come in, Mr. O'Francis."

Her handshake was firm for the size of the body she had. She was a very petite woman with a warm smile, an attractive face, short dark-brown hair, and a well-proportioned body.

"Have a seat," she said as she pointed to the two chairs facing her desk.

"Okay, now, I understand you have a problem with a letter that your boss sent out to a variety of people?"

"Yes, that is correct, but ex-boss."

"Do you have the letter with you?"

"Yes, I do." Jim reached into his briefcase and withdrew a folder that contained several pieces of paper. "Here is what I would consider a very damaging letter. I have been advised that it is very defamatory."

"Who did you show this letter to for you to come to this conclusion?"

"I showed it to three attorneys, Mr. Philps, Mr. Starnoc, and Mr. Fitzroy."

She took a few minutes to read the letter and then laid the letter in front of her on the desk.

"Mr. O'Francis, they were correct. It is a damaging letter. Now, what do you want to do about it?"

Jim took a few seconds to collect his thoughts. "Well, "Ms. Donatello, I want to know what I can do, legally, that is, about this. And madam, I would like to say that this is only the tip of the iceberg. I mean, well … it is a very long story, and …"

"No, no, Mr. O'Francis, I would like to hear about some of your problems. That way, I can understand why such a letter was written in the first place."

He pulled out his yellow legal pad, where he had bulleted an extensive outline of events in chronological order by date and year. For the next hour and a half, James Patrick gave her a very brief synopsis about some of his problems and the incident at the corner gas station, and then went back to his last year at the high school working under the twisted mind of an evil dictator. He included what he had done to Dawn and his son Michael.

"Okay, Mr. O'Francis, may I call you Jim?"

"Sure."

"You may call me Holly. Now, I will take your case. I will need two thousand dollars up front as a retainer fee."

"Okay," he replied.

"Now, wait one minute, just what figure were you thinking about when we file the suit?"

"Figure?" Jim asked.

"Yes, how much were you thinking about suing for, and Jim, I will receive thirty-three and a third percent of whatever we get from the case if we win."

"Well, I do not know," he stated.

"Well, you must have had some figure in mind, didn't you?"

"Yes, I did, but... "

"But what?" Holly quickly responded, with an all-business tone in her voice.

"Well, I would like to file a suit for one million dollars!"

A moment of silence as Holly sat back in her chair, her arms on the arms of her chair, never taking her eyes off Jim, something Jim had taken note of and liked right away about her. She was not afraid to make eye contact and hold it; *rare for women*, he thought. But, of course, he was not exposed to Holly's caliber of women. He had been surrounded by women teachers for the past fifteen years.

"Jim, I do not think we can get that around here. If you were out east or up north in a more metropolitan area, you could tap into the million-dollar area, but it is unrealistic for this part of the country. I was thinking ... let me ... how about half a million for the two of them?"

The statement caught Jim a bit off guard. "What do you mean the two of them?"

"I believe that we will name both Bales and Finkel in the suit, as they both have conspired to create this letter." Jim looked puzzled at her use of the word *conspired*.

"Jim, keep in mind that from what you have told me, and I can at this point only assume that you are telling the truth, Richard Finkel had to take the information from the gas station to Damon Bales, and that means that they had to conspire to write the letter."

"Correct! And Ms. Donatello, I am not in any way, form, or fashion lying! You can be assured that if I tell you something, it is a fact! If you ask me something, I will, and have always stated it just like it is! My word reflects me. I am a man of my word! My word is the very reason I have had so much trouble in the school system in which I have worked. But you would not know anything about that." Jim's voice had become slightly defensive.

"I believe you, and I have it from a good source that you are a man of your word." She stood and stuck her hand out to Jim across the desk.

"Jim, you would probably be amazed at what I know about your school system. I know Dan Jakes very well. I will let my secretary draw up the proper papers. Now let us set a date for the next appointment. Let's say next Tuesday. What is a good time for you?"

"I do not get out of school until 1530, I mean ..."

"Oh, that is fine. I understand military time. I served several years in the army as an attorney, so you are on good ground with me with that. Okay, let's say 1630 hours."

"Fine, I will be here with a check for two thousand, correct?"

"Correct. And Jim, I also will need all your files, written documentation, and taped conversations, and a list of people you think I will need to talk to."

Jim was not happy with the half-million figure as he traveled home, but he was not a lawyer, so he would assume she knew what she was talking about. Still, a million, he felt, would have buckled their knees. *Moreover, she was a JAG officer. Wow, now I want to see them handle her*, Jim thought, and then a smile came across his face.

Connections

He had been a Vietnam War veteran, attached to a SOG unit, "spooks," as they were called. The CIA had their hooks in him, and he had spent several years doing the covert, not-so-legal work for our government, the kind of work (the spy game) that *they* did not do.

His government had betrayed him, or one should say by one of the government's elected political figures, one of the "good" senators.

Technically, he was dead. His CIA identity was dead. Only three people knew he had survived the hit on him. As far as the CIA knew, officially, he was dead. His body had never been completely recovered. All that remained was a pile of ashes and a few broken bones that had been scattered about as if someone had been searching for something—the victim of a blown-up, burned-out car and pieces of a body. For identification, the best anyone in the agency could come up with was that all evidence pointed to the

American agent was dead, according to the official report presented by the CIA.

They had lost a good agent because of one of the government's many corrupt senators. And this one was indebted and embedded with a Russian spy with a cover story of being in the financial world of wall street.

The affair he had been having for the past five years that neither his wife and family nor anyone else of importance knew about was a side issue. It was always just another junket he had to take for two or three days. But of course, what the idiot senator did not know was the woman was working for the Russian syndicate and had with great ease dug her nails in so deep, he would never get off the hook. Unless he died, but the illicit money and the secret life, the excitement, the thrill of it all kept him going. But of course, the game's name was money and a lot of it, which was typical of Washington politicians.

A dead agent needs a new identity, a new location, a new job, a job related to his investigation expertise, gathering information, spying, eavesdropping, photographing, and if necessary, assassinating whom he chose.

A few law firms in the local area would hire him to do what he had done in the spy world he had lived in for many years, gathering information on someone. Or, as it was referred to, assets. But now, he could do it at his pleasure, not for the government. In addition, with less dangerous cases/assignments. He did not need a job for money. He would never have to worry about money for the remainder of his life. That had been taken care of long before his "sudden departure from this earth." He took precautions and ensured that his future was well-financed with Swiss and Cayman bank accounts and several accounts in the United States under several names.

He planned carefully. His Italian name would have to go in the vault; no more Mario Sagaria Rosso. He would need a new identity; he would take his middle name, which translated into Paul. He had a Viet Nam friend by the name of O'Neill. It sounded good. His olive-tone skin and dark hair would be from his mother's side of the family if an explanation were ever needed. It was called a backstop. To make sure an agent's cover is not blown. But of course, the "cover within a cover" (in case the backstop did not work) was always ready. He needed an obscure place, small in size yet large enough not to stand out. He traveled for weeks from northeastern Canada through the New England states, finally settling in the eastern mountains of Tennessee.

His new lifestyle would be for enjoyment. So, Paul spent a few years buying land on top of a mountain, building a road, and designing and building the house he had always wanted. He had learned the lay of the nearby city, the culture and types of people, and businesses in the area. He came to realize that he had chosen well. A lot of Irish-Italian rooted families lived throughout the entire region. However, after all the work was done and all the asset gathering, he had become bored, so he quietly started his own PI business. Most of his work was minor jobs, not very exciting. Still, he had in his life all the excitement he needed between his Viet Nam experiences and his postwar "I Spy" experience, which was enough to last a lifetime.

Twenty years after his "death," and in his fifties, the dull life of a small city PI checking on who was cheating on whom or a little work for some local

attorney on some civil cases here and there was all
Paul needed. He had gotten to assist the local police in
a few homicides.

He had kept right much to himself, not getting
personally close to people and the ones with whom he
picked to converse outside of business. He was
meticulous, not letting people, in general, know
anything about his past, which was none of anyone's
business anyway. But small towns and small-city
people were gossipy and nosey. Not that much
different than "Big Brother." He was not fond of most
reporters. But over the years of experience of
following stories in the newspapers, he concluded that
they always claimed absence of malice.

Paul's connection to Joseph Caprotti came
about by accident, a case he had been working on for
several months. Finally, through some covert
checking, he got all the information he needed about
Joseph Caprotti and his connections to the Spadalini
Family in Chicago. The local prosecuting attorney had
sought his small business out for much-needed
assistance in solving a homicide case involving a

wealthy local pillar of the community. The prosecutor had figured some small outside private firm could get enough leads that he could crack the case and get some big headlines, with a possible future political advancement attached to his excellent work. However, he had picked the wrong PI firm, and the information Paul had discovered was worth more to him than to the prosecuting attorney. So, he sorrowfully reported that all leads had dead-ended, leaving the police and the prosecuting attorney's office with a cold case.

After more intelligence gathering on Joseph Caprotti and who he was and who he worked for, Paul traveled to Chicago. After making professional contact with Joseph and a lengthy luncheon meeting, Paul gave Joseph the inside information concerning the cold-case assassination. Unfortunately for Joseph, Paul also provided details about Joseph and his father-in-law, Vincent Spadalini, making him uncomfortable.

Joseph arranged a meeting with Vincent Spadalini and Paul with Joseph sitting in. The first meeting lasted several hours and then extended over several days of meetings. Vincent learned what Paul wanted him to know and nothing about his "other" life or birth name. Paul provided Vincent with information concerning him and his business and some influential people connected to his shipping business that Vincent thought no one knew. Sharing such privileged intelligence validated a bonded alliance between Paul and Vincent and a business partnership. After several years had passed, Paul was hired to do some work for the "Family Spadalini," and the bond and trust grew tighter. For the most part, Spadalini and his businesses were legal. For the most part. But that could also apply to the government, for the most part. In many cases, Vincent's businesses were even cleaner than the organization Paul had previously worked for, his dear "uncle."

"Uncle Sam" was by no means legal in its day-to-day operations and all its agencies and splinter agencies that no one knew about. Therefore, Paul was not so quick to judge Joseph Caprotti and his connection to Vincent and the Spadalini family as to any of their business operations or their methods of dealing with business problems. Yet, he had seen, done, and was very well aware of much worse by "The Company" and the United States government, which was sworn to uphold the nation's accepted social norms, mores, and laws.

⛎

The phone rang three times before the answering machine picked up. "Blue Ridge Investigation, leave your name and number, and I will get back to you."

"This is Joseph. Call me."

He had done a few jobs for Joseph and the Spadalini "Family," nothing "head-line" catching, information-gathering on a few people, a few pictures, some daily schedules, routes, and habits. It did not matter the reason or the outcome to Paul. He would not get directly involved. Just do the job he was hired for and let it go. No one knew who he was, and he was not getting on the front page of any newspaper, no pictures of him, and no comments from him. So he kept a low profile, and he would keep it that way, just a tiny city PI.

His residence was a remote, lovely mountain cabin with all the luxuries one could ask for, along with electronic equipment and security. He kept a small apartment in the small city as a cover and often stayed there. He bought an entire building, renovated it to his liking, and rented the lower half out to an antique dealer. His office was on the second floor overlooking the corner of Main and Commonwealth, in the middle of downtown, in a not-so-fancy but classic building constructed in the early 1920s.

He sat in his worn, high-backed wooden office chair, his feet resting on the low part of a very wide windowsill, typical of the era, a foot or so off the floor. Looking out one of the two windows, one on each side of the corner of his office, he rocked back and forth, thinking, holding his coffee cup with both hands to his lips, and occasionally taking a sip. The windows were tall and wide, with original glass panes still in them, another telltale sign of a less complex era.

He thought about the 1920s, an era of good feeling. *I think I would have liked to have lived during that* era. So he thought as he took another sip of hot coffee. He liked the old Art Deco–style office building and the old office style. He had the entire building professionally cleaned and repairs done where needed. He had a company come in and clean every inch of the interior of the building before he or anyone else moved in. He kept the old, dark hardwood floors, worn with use over the many years, the old windows and windowsills worn with the dark-brown color showing the wear of a time when there were no air conditioners; the doors in the office, solid oak, dark brown almost black in color. He kept the original solid-brass doorknobs and long key plates. He refused to remove the old windows and had contracted custom-fitted storm windows to go over the original ones, making his office and the rest of the building's windows energy efficient. There was something about the building that made Paul feel comfortable.

He had the ceiling painted white, which did brighten up the room. The walls were plaster covered and by all accounts were original, so he had repairs done to them where needed, and they were yellow-stained, so he had them professionally cleaned, leaving them a cream color, with a somewhat rough texture.

He would take a sip of coffee and look down on the early morning busy street below as he listened to the message on the answering machine. It was 9:40 a.m., and Mary J. (Fitzpatrick) Pendergrass, his secretary, arrived. Mary J. was a five-foot-three inch, 145-pound, fifty-five-year-old divorced mother of two grown children. Her arrival as the firm's only secretary came a month after Paul had opened his office doors.

Mary was looking for work and stopped at the antique corner store, inquiring about any employment. Jonathan and Lisa Williams, a couple in their sixties, had been operating the store for four months and were having success, primarily due to the excellent location. As they needed no assistance, they directed Mary to the upstairs business and their landlord, as they thought Paul was looking for a secretary.

Her daily schedule was to stop by the post office to pick up the mail, as he had no mail delivered to his office. His office had two rooms, a large outer office, and his rather large office. The rest of the entire upstairs was just space and closed off. The door was slightly open. He could hear her getting a cup of coffee, as he had already made it, which meant he had arrived early. Mary started to go through the mail. He turned and reached for the phone, opened a blue address book, turned to the letter C, and dialed Joseph Caprotti's number. On the third ring, Joseph picked up.

"Hello."

"Joseph, returning your call."

"Good morning. How are things in the South?"

"They are fine. The weather is nice. What can I do for you?"

"I need some information on a friend." A pause of silence on the line. He had never asked for information on "a friend," a particular person, yes, but Joseph had never used the word *friend* seeking any work that was needed.

"By chance, do you know where James Patrick is located?" Another long pause of silence.

"Ahh, no. He moved some time ago with no forwarding address."

"I need to get in touch with him. No trouble, I need to talk to him. I will hire you to locate him. I will pay you our arranged fee for your time and expense."

"What is so important in locating him?"

"I owe him a few favors, and I would like to talk to him concerning some details about what I owe him."

"Joseph, I don't know if he wants to be found."

"I think he would want to hear what I have to tell him. Business, you understand?"

"Yes … I understand. Joseph … you know how I feel about him. He has gone through enough, don't want him to suffer any undue hardships!"

"I know … nor do I. He won't. I give you my word."

"I'll hold you to that!"

"I know you will. Again…I assure you no malice is here. No grief will come to him or the remainder of his family."

"Vincent."

"He approved."

"I'll see what I can do. I'll get back to you."

☿

Big Sky Country

Montana had always appealed to Jim, not so for Dawn. But Jim wanted open areas, very few people, and he could find what he was looking for there. On the other hand, the weather was not to his liking, especially the winters. That was the part that Dawn would not have liked. She hated cold weather, and Montana winters were no fun. Still, he would choose Mother Nature's harsh winters between the tragic events in his life and the local corrupt political machines, their self-righteous norms, and the people associated with them.

The remoteness of the northwestern mountain state and its rugged topography ensured that the area was one of the last areas settled by the Europeans, one of the last areas anyone would look for him.

Fort Missoula, Montana, a good-sized town just east of Bitterroot Mountain, sat where the Clark, Bitterroot, and Blackfoot rivers joined. To the north of Fort Missoula was Flathead Indian country, a large lake named Flathead Lake in honor of the Native

American tribe. He moved west of Fort Missoula, about five miles off O'Brien Road, a good Irish name, so he knew it had to be a good place. Jim O'Francis bought a small ranch with over two thousand acres of land, small compared to some of the area ranches but average for the state.

The place had a lovely modern one-story log house with many windows and big rooms. Four bedrooms, more than he needed, but he would always have a room for his oldest and only living son and only grandson, from his youngest son Patrick, and at least one guest room when they visited. He liked lots of space, and he even had a room that was just big enough for his private dojo, as his karate was part of his everyday life and would remain so as long as he could stretch daily and do a few katas. Jim hated to be cramped into a small place. The living room or great room was huge and open, with a large front window allowing a picturesque view. It featured a massive rock fireplace that he used every chance he got, and of course, during the late fall, winter, and early spring, that was almost daily.

Jim loved the smell of the wood as he sat in his rocking chair, with the flickering of the fire in the darkness of his great room late at night. The house had wood flooring except for the three bathrooms with ceramic tile flooring. The kitchen was as modern as any in the country, with its white marble floors, lots of space to move about, and many cabinets. It had an island in the middle, which was something Dawn would have wanted. A few items O'Francis replaced and upgraded were the stove and refrigerator. He got a commercial gas stove, a double-door refrigerator, and a double-door commercial freezer, all in stainless steel.

Dawn always wanted that for her dream kitchen, which was her domain. Over the years they had been together, she always cooked up something different and used Jim as her guinea pig. She was an excellent cook and could have hosted her own cooking show (something she enjoyed watching on TV) if she had wanted.

Jim installed a large heat pump that kept the house temperature constant year-round.

Jim added a large deck to the back of the house. He loved decks and enjoyed spending time on them, looking off in the distance at the mountain range in the evening as the sunset. He knew that the real estate agent never did understand why he insisted that the house he would buy had to face the east and the back to the west. But it did not matter if the agent understood or not; it was a Masonic thing, and most people would never understand anyway.

It had a nice oversized three-car garage and a paved drive for a quarter of a mile to the main county road that led directly into town. The yard was about the right size, one hundred by two hundred feet in the front and one hundred by one hundred feet in the back. There were about fifty feet on each side of the house. It had a natural wood fence around the entire house, separating it from the farmland.

The barn was just what the doctor ordered, about one hundred yards from the house. The roof was shaped like a bent horseshoe with forty-five-degree angles extending from the top, and the top had a stripe running the entire length of the barn, about two feet wide, made of thick Plexiglas, letting in lots of light. The barn had an open area extending from one end to the other with eight stalls, four on each side. It also had a stall for storage, such as grain (sweet feed, corn) for the horses on the left side. An open area in the loft running the barn's length on both sides was

[148]

used for storing hay. It had a large stall for saddles and all the tack equipment used for horse riding. Jim added two features to the barn as soon as he settled in and reorganized it. First, electricity was added, allowing lots of lights and outlets. Second, he added water facilities to the barn and a faucet at each end, and a water hose connected to each one would extend the barn's length if needed.

He redid the horse stalls' floors by having them concreted with drains put in each, extending the drains out to one large septic tank separate from the house septic tank. This flooring would allow Jim to keep his barn clean, and he felt like his four horses also liked it. Whether they did or not, or for that matter, if they cared less, he thought they did, and that was how he was. At each end of the barn was a sliding door to close off the winter cold and allow the horses to enter the barn from the field side and not have to come out to the house side. James P. added a wooden gate to the front side to allow airflow through the barn in good weather. The horses got used to coming in and going to their stalls. Often they would just stand in the open area of the middle of the barn or look out over the gate at the front of the barn. Jim kept water in four stalls for the four horses he owned.

His favorite horse was a buckskin breed with perfect black markings. He communicated well with his animals, and they seemed to understand. A natural wood-treated fence from the front edge of the barn extended some fifty yards out in both directions and then back toward an open field for about two hundred yards square with a gate in the middle area. His entire land boundary was fenced with four runs of barbed wire. It had been subdivided into two hundred acres for grazing, a hundred for spring grass, and a hundred for fall grass. A hundred was fenced off for growing hay for his livestock and about sixty for corn. The remaining grazing land had a medium-sized creek running through the northwestern part, giving his stock access to all the water they would need. A four-wheeler path had been made around the entire fenced boundary, as horseback repair had been outdated by time and machines. His stock was not of the cattle variety, like the rest of the local ranchers', but of the magnificent American Bison. They did not need any real care in any season. Unlike the cow, the Bison could graze on the land year-round.

In the harshest winters, Jim made sure they had hay to eat but left them to graze off the land, allowing them to remain independent and dependent on the land, as they had done for a thousand years. He had long loved the Bison's greatness and all it stood for. Jim had always wanted Bison Ranch, and he started with a herd of fifty, intending to sell off about ten to twenty as the herd grew for-profit and meat in his freezer. He had two bulls to populate his herd. The females gave berth to calves in the spring, April or May. One per female; on a rare occasion, you might have a set of twins born.

With the help of two locals he had hired, Jim had no problem keeping his herd up. He did not need the money anymore and often gave meat away to the needy and organizations that helped the needs of the less fortunate.

It had not been his teaching profession's retirement that had left him financially secure, which he had automatically deposited in a bank in a small town in northern New England. His foresight in some investments paid off beyond his wildest imagination, leaving him set for life. He had used his newfound wealth wisely and had reinvested in areas that would bring in a steady income, plus his ranch, which he estimated would only net him around forty thousand a year. Not a lot to compare with the surrounding ranchers, but he did not need his land to survive economically. He needed it to survive mentally. None of his Montana ranches came from teaching retirement money, which was a joke. He had invested very wisely with his "pot of gold." He had turned a mere few hundred thousand into ten million, thanks to a booming economy through the late nineties and the turn of the century.

He had pulled all his money out of the high-risk investments and had it secured in a safe but less profit-making account before the market took its dive. None of what he now enjoyed could have been possible if it were not for a little Irish luck and intelligent investments. No one outside his family knew of his windfall, and he would keep it that way. The illegal stash fund he had so carefully buried a few years before his final move, he had recovered. He had discreetly placed it in three separate bank safety deposit boxes in another small northern New England town. He had his phone unlisted and unpublished with a list of everyone with his number. His mail was delivered to a P.O. Box, with only his initial J. and last name.

Jim had stayed up late looking at the stars in hopes of seeing something other than a meteorite, but as usual, nothing unusual crossed his sight, so he went to bed around 0100 hours. He was asleep in a matter of minutes, what seemed to be a long time, but was only a short forty-five minutes. Jim awoke suddenly to a voice. He looked carefully around the bedroom with his eyes, not moving his head or body. Slowly he reached across his body to his nightstand to his left (he always slept on the left side of the bed) and grasped his .357 firmly in his right hand. His two friends, he always would say, Mr. Smith and Mr. Wesson, were always close by his side. Jim saw nothing. He heard nothing. It was not another Nam dream. The ghosts of his past had not come calling in a long time. And even when they arrived, it was rare. He accepted his part in history and learned to live with it. He contributed that he did not have the thrill of reliving the war over and over, night after night, to the fact of not being under stress and the constant battle protecting his name with unscrupulous school administrators and a corrupt political system. What's in a name? His was priceless.

But the voice was so clear, so plain. It was not Dawn. It was not Patrick. He knew their voices. He always knew when they visited, which left him feeling warm and happy. He got up and went to his favorite rocking chair to think, to try and recall what he had heard or dreamed and why. It had been "The Man." Why? He had not thought of him in several years. How did he know he needed to contact him, and why? James Patrick knew that he did not know where he was. Jim also knew that Paul knew that he had not told him the truth about where he was going. But it was something Jim had to do, and Jim knew that Paul, of all people, would have understood. Jim had told only two men where he was going and did not go where he had stated he would.

Not even his only living son, Michael, and his wife Maria, his daughter-in-law Leigh O'Francis, who never remarried after the loss of Patrick, no one knew where he was. As far as James P. knew, it included "the men." Jim left all believing he had indeed relocated to the mountains of northern Georgia at the foothills of the Great Appalachian Mountain chain along the North Carolina border. He hated lying to them, but his little voice advised him to do so, and he always listened to his internal voice. James P. would have to give this subconscious voice much thought. So, he put it aside and went back to bed. He was awake just as the dawn was breaking. He heard the same voice and the same message. He rose, got dressed, and by 0700 hours, he informed the spirit of Dawn that he was going for a ride and would be back in a couple of hours.

The early morning ride was not something out of the ordinary. Jim needed the fresh air, the sound of nature, and the smell of his horse. *Yes,* he thought, *this will help clear my thoughts up.*

The air had a slight chill, so he wore his favorite cowhide coat, lined in sheep wool that extended over the sleeves and collar. He wore a pair of tan goatskin gloves, Lee jeans, a blue long-sleeve shirt, brown western boots, and a leather, flat-brimmed cowboy hat. He would ride out to talk to his American icons. The Native Americans seemed to get along for centuries with the idea of communicating with nature and the Bison. Long before the "good Christian religions" and their holier-than-thou carriers of the "true word," they declared that the Native Americans were wrong. But, of course, the Caucasian European worldwide organized Christian religion had the inside track on communicating with "Their" God, not the Great Spirit.

Being the excellent agent Paul was, he knew that Jim was not where he said he would be, or for that matter, in the same area. Something he would have done in his case. Paul ran every check he knew and covered every possibility of locating Jim in the area and the state of Georgia. He was not in the Volunteer State, nor was he in the Tar Heel State. He knew he would have never relocated to the Commonwealth of Virginia. West Virginia did not suit him. He never did like it. Kentucky was too flat from the middle and west, and the eastern part was too close to Virginia. South Carolina was too flat. Now the question was, where did he go?

Did he leave any clues in his conversations with him over the years? Would he go to the northeast? Maybe. The mountains of Vermont, maybe New

Hampshire, but no further north. It made him proud of Jim. *Paul thought he most likely would have made an outstanding agent. He sure had all the qualifications for it. I am glad he didn't let the government get its hooks into him. He would have been fucked just like I was!*

The bitterness surfaced in Paul for the first time in many years, his contempt for the people running the nation, their pompous, self-righteous attitude, and their attitude toward the agency. *God*, he thought, *fucking politicians can fuck up a one-car funeral!*

He would need a little help in finding James Patrick. He was unsure he wanted to, as he labored over why he was getting paid. However, he needed to locate him for several reasons, of course, Joseph's request, which he felt he knew. Paul had spent three weeks looking for Jim.

He decided to go to his mountain home. It was time to rest and get some help from some old friends. He had not contacted the only two people who knew he was in existence for at least two years.

The United States was a big place, and one could disappear in it and never be found unless one had the right connections, and then, over time, about anyone could be found unless you were dead. But even then, if cremated, ashes scatted to the wind, you cannot be located.

It was late or early, depending on one's point of view of the night, 0200 hours. He went to his basement with its wall-to-wall shelves of hundreds of old and new hardbound books, antique bottles, jars, wooden carvings, and a few bronze busts and statues between the many books. The walled shelves were one of three, all looking the same. He walked to the thermostat next to the glass doors leading outside. He moved the bottom lever on the thermostat to the off position and then moved the top lever to forty-five degrees. On the opposite side of the room, an entire section of the bookshelves made a click and a slight movement inward. He walked across the room to where a tiny opening had appeared. One could see a hairline of light along the wall. He lightly pushed the bookshelf and stepped into a well-lighted room. He then moved the door wall until it clicked closed. The thermostat levers returned to their original position.

An utterly soundproof room, measuring thirty by thirty feet with no windows, was located under the two-car garage. The concrete walls and ceiling measured four inches thick. An antique desk sat somewhere close to the middle of the room. A phone and one notepad were all that was on the desk. One would have thought they had entered a war room in the Pentagon.

To the back of the desk against the wall were two long antique wooden tables with two computers and reel-to-reel tape players, two printers, a fax machine, a typewriter, and a shredder on a separate antique table to the right side of the desk. Against the wall were eight surveillance monitors, a keyboard to their controls, and a small antique desk with two other phones with a square black box with a place for the phone receiver to fit into them. He went to one of the phones at the small desk, took it off the hook, placed it on the black box, and then dialed a number.

After three rings, a sleepy voice on the other end of the line answered, "Hello."

"JFK."

Then a pause came, and a response, "Jacqueline Bouvier."

"Camelot," Paul spoke. Then came another response.

"It never rains until after sundown. Ahh, Paul, do you know what time it is?"

"Of course I do. It is time that we talk. Are we secure?" Paul inquired.

"Yes ... but let me double check. Hold on." A pause. "Secure," came the response on the other end of the line. "What have you been up to? I have not heard from you in over two years."

"Ah ... a little work here and there, nothing earthshaking. Keeping busy. How is everything in the castle?"

"The same old, same old ... have you talked to King Arthur?"

"No, but would you have him call me on three if you talk to him today? I will be here all day. I need a little help from you on a very covert matter."

"What are you into?"

"No, nothing major, just a little assistance in locating a friend, and could use some high-tech sources."

"Okay, what say we call this afternoon around 1600? Ahh, a great number." Then he laughed.

"Yes, it is. I will talk to you then and fill you and Arthur in on what I need."

"Good deal. Later." The phone clicked on the other end of the line. Paul sat and listened for thirty seconds before he disconnected his phone and looked over to the reel-to-reel to see if it was still recording.

The Legal System

After several meetings with Holly, she formulated a plan of action. Finally, it was March, and Jim felt he would get some form of justice. So Holly went to the Reynolds County Courthouse and filed a half-million-dollar lawsuit against Damon Bales and Richard Finkel. She had timed filing the proper papers so it would be closing time and had made all the arrangements for a US Marshal to serve the documents on Monday to Bales and Finkel at Honsburg High. It would give Jim a great deal of pleasure knowing the shock of being sued and the embarrassment from all the Gang of Jackals hanging around the office.

But again, James Patrick would not get that tiny bit of joy. Saturday morning, Jarvis Griffith, the clerk of Reynolds County and a personal friend and political comrade of Damon's, phoned him and summoned him to his office.

"There is something you need to see." The two men walked to the courthouse doors, and Griffith unlocked and opened the door.

"What is it?"

"Wait, I will show you. I want to let you see. I don't want to tell you." Jarvis locked the doors behind him, went to his office, pulled out the paperwork on the suit, and handed it to Damon. He looked over the front page and was halfway down the page before speaking.

"That sonofabitch! Goddamanit, I hate that bastard! Damn... I wish we would have gone along with the plan to eliminate the sonofabitch! Now, what the hell am I to do?"

"I have someone who will take care of the problem. The first thing to do is do nothing until the papers are served. Then we can put things to work. Shit, Damon, don't worry; we will take care of you. Hell, everyone knows he is a piece of shit and has caused nothing but trouble for us for years. This is nothing to worry yourself. It will be handled."

"What about Finkel?"

"Well ... that is another matter. It depends on how things unfold. Let's wait and see. I'll let Duncan,

Marshy, and Daniel know what is happening. You call Bobby, then let Richard know. He worries me a little, but at any rate, we'll talk later."

Monday came, and Marshals Woodward and Holbrook arrived and requested to see Bales and Finkel. Damon was, of course, expecting him and had a bit of a shit-eating grin on his face as Marshal Holbrook handed him the papers, informing him he had been duly served. He then asked to see Richard Finkel. The two marshals were told that Mr. Finkel was not at work. Indeed he was not. Richard Finkel missed the next two days covered by Damon and Marshy and was not charged for missing work, but the Marshal found his home, waited for him to arrive, and served him with the papers Wednesday night.

It was Saturday, and the gang met at Marshy's home, as it was set back into the forest and on a small hill. No one could see the cars from the main road. They had a nice dinner of steak and all the trimmings of a big meal as they sat and discussed O'Francis' move, "high-level meeting," as O'Francis would have referred to it. A judge, a clerk of the court, a superintendent of schools, a high school principal, a county supervisor, and a leading political figure with many powerful political connections. The primary power players were in place to determine the fate of one lowly, simple teacher and ex-coach. In the course of a lengthy meeting, a tiny thorn that they were about to pull out and dispose of, Damon stated in his mass of ignorance, "I think we should have gone through with my suggestion a long time ago. Eliminate him. Hell, it would have cost us a lot less than it is going to."

A silence came over the group, and then Daniel spoke. "But it is less dangerous getting him in this manner. We have more control of events this way, less worry."

Marshy chimed in. "Look, don't worry about the money, Damon. It will be handled. A minor glitch won't cost you a dime. Hell, he is the one that will pay out of his pocket. I can assure you of that!"

Irvin stood, stretched, and walked to the window.

"You know we have done about everything to the bastard and still can't drive him out. He knows too much. It is my opinion he is dangerous. Most people would have given it up and left the area. It bothers me why he does not come open with what he knows. I know he is aware of some of our activities, and I am a little more than concerned about what I don't know what he knows. I just don't understand why he has not tried to, shall I say, blackmail us with what he has?"

Damon responded quickly. "That is fine. He had another son in junior high. One way or the other, gentlemen, one way or the other... it will be done!"

Irvin then turned to face his comrades. "LaMar, how in the hell does he find out all the little things he does, or seems to be always dropping words here and there in the conversations with certain people in the community that he knows will tell us what he has stated or questioned? I don't know how many people have come to me and asked me questions about any one of us and items concerning the school system and conversations in private. I am getting fed up with explaining these damn questions to these dumbasses. It is becoming more frequent. It is always what Coach

[166]

O'Francis said or told me. Fuck him! I want to know how he knows what the hell is going on inside the system! Our business! I want to find the leak! And I want the leak fired! Or, well."

"Calm down, Irvin. Shit, it will be handled."

"Well, LaMar, when? I mean, you have been handling O'Francis now for four goddamn years! He is still here and is still challenging the policies as well as the administrators, and again, still sending messages."

"Hey, look, we have hurt him a lot. He is down, and I know it. He'll never coach again anywhere. I am damn sure that he will never teach again outside this county. He is financially hurting, and I know that. These things take time. You have said that yourself."

"Yeah, but most people..."

"He's not most people."

"Ahh, no shit!"

Damon spoke. "Well, you all don't have to work with him daily."

LaMar laughed loudly and then stated, "And nor do you anymore. Bobby will have to deal with him again. He is but a small problem. Now, boys, everyone knows I don't have anything for Bobby, and I know several of you like him, and that is fine. But, let's all pull together here. There is more at stake here than O'Francis, and we all know what I mean. Let's not let this thing get out in the open. We do not want any state and damn sure do not want any federal investigation into alleged illegal activity within our system and community. We must keep this thing within our boundaries to control whatever may occur. Everyone here likes the cash flow. So, let's not get ahead of our skies." They looked at LaMar as to state, *"What the fuck does that mean."*

There were several minutes of silence in the room.

"Another thing, before we move on to more important items. Has anyone questioned why O'Francis has not gone to the feds? I mean, look, he has dropped enough hints to us that he knows, and you wonder why I have become extremely concerned. Damon just may have the right solution."

Again, silence permeated the room as each one began looking at the others.

Talking to Jim

I followed O'Francis and his saga, as I have done now for many years, and he continues to surprise me. I asked him in the spring of 1990, "Why don't you move? Jim, you have criminal indictment material on the political powers in the county. But, on the other hand, go public. You have a ton of information about the illegal, covert money-making businesses they are involved in and all their connections."

He thought for maybe thirty seconds. "Because I have a younger son to get through this piece of shit of a public school system first, and it is not right for me to move because I am having problems with the political power players in the county, as to going public. I will not place my family in harm's way. I know how the game is played, and I know who the real players are, and I know that even though *they* think *they* are big fish in a big ocean, they are just big fish in a tiny pond."

I looked directly at Jim with a very puzzled look on my face with that statement. I thought I knew what he was talking about. Yet, he had never revealed anything to me about any connections he might have with any organization or anyone who might even be remotely connected to any organization or influential, wealthy people.

He continued. "Patrick did not ask to come into this world, and it is up to me to give him every opportunity to make it. And moving from here to start in another place is not good. It would not be fair to him since he is already established. It is challenging for a teen to relocate, make new friends, and be accepted. Hell, I still have not been accepted in Honsburg! But these people do not know that my grandfather, great-grandfather, and great-great-grandfather Stout are from this town. Even before it was legally incorporated, I will put up with the petty bullshit and fight these bastards with every breath I have until my sons have completed their education, as piss poor as the system is!

"As to the second question, I cannot see the legal system doing anything about what information I have. Even though it is highly illegal, what they are doing and have done, there are just too many holes in the cheese for me to go public. And if by going public, you mean the media, well, I trust them just about as much as I do the political and legal system. For the media, there is no absence of malice. Not enough protection for my family or me."

Then he paused and walked across the room. "I am not at all sure that the legal system is legal. However, I know you figure that I have more information than I am telling you, and you are correct in your thoughts. Correct?"

I did not respond right away, and there was a very long period of silence. Then, "Yes, you are correct, Jim. However, I also figured that you would have told me if you wanted me to know."

James Patrick turned to face me across the room. He just smiled. "You are a reporter."

I quickly stated, "Retired."

He slowly answered, "However, still a reporter. Maybe not a media type, but journalists are just as uncaring as the media. Just as hungry for a story. They are looking for that journalistic award that sets them apart from all others. Putting them at the top of the pill, that coveted award that somebody gives to whomever for the best story of the year."

"Jim, I have given you my word as to what I will get printed and when you tell me it is okay to do so, and not a letter until. I value my words just as much as you do. We do have something in common."

James Patrick stood in silence, looking at me. I did not continue with what I mistakenly let slip. He never asked. He just stood there looking directly at me, the electrodes in his mind firing at a supersonic speed, as to what we had in common.

Umpiring Begins

Jim contacted the baseball commissioner in February of '90 to take his test, recertify himself to umpire high school games, and let him know he would be available to call that year. Edward Lowe had just two years earlier, when O'Francis was still coaching baseball talked to him about umpiring when he was through with his coaching duties.

Ed informed Jim, "When you get out of this business, you will have been on record as an umpire."

He told Jim he would have at least three years on record as a certified umpire to call postseason games. So, O'Francis took the test and certified himself as an official baseball umpire in the spring of 1988. In addition, he had provided the commissioner and the umpiring association with his records of umpiring high school baseball while living "up north," which included postseason games and his ratings from the umpires association.

"Damon and company may stop you from coaching someday, but they will not be successful in keeping you out of baseball." James Patrick remembered the statement and wondered if Edward had some foresight into his life. Jim would be removed as a baseball coach within two years.

☿

Kevin Barnard and Arthur MacFraley entered their senior year of baseball without Coach O'Francis. He had been their strength; he had made believers out of them. When Coach O'Francis was present, the battery of Barnard and MacFraley could not be beaten, or so they felt. Jim would call every pitch for them, leaving the pitching and catching jobs without worrying whether they had made the correct pitch for the batter. They knew their coach would take the heat for a wrong call for a particular pitch. And some batter went "yard" on them. So, O'Francis would tell them constantly, "Do not worry about a hit or a home run. You concentrate on your job. I will take care of the rest." So they did, and they were good; they felt good, and they believed in themselves.

Not only did O'Francis know the game, but he also knew what made players like Barnard and

MacFraley tick. He was able to communicate with them on life's real problems. He was able to reach them with their "own big problems" as teens and put them in a manner they could understand. They would come to him with what they considered issues— teachers, grades, girlfriends, and parents, even the head coach. Then, when they left, O'Francis made it all fit into the scheme of life's day-in and day-out education. Things did not seem so bad after a long talk with Coach O'Francis.

Jim O'Francis' absence from the Honsburg baseball team left Barnard having a lousy year altogether, as there was no one to help him control his temper and no one to understand his emotions. No one could calm him down, and he lost his edge. He could not concentrate when he was on the mound. Arthur had lost his sharpness as a catcher. He was not as confident in his throws to second. He had passed balls that a season earlier he would have never had— no one to "whisper" in his ear about the fundamental teachings. No time was taken to stop everything and instruct. No encouraging word of wisdom was expressed to either of them when needed. They were just eighteen years old and still needed guidance.

Teddy Hauler did not give them what they needed in terms of confidence. He talked a lot, but his words made no difference. It was not that Ted did not try; he did. It was just not the same. Tim Harper knew the game but did not know the players. He could not communicate with them on the level they had been accustomed to. Harper was never the communicator. He had never been the coach who could make believers out of the players. They missed the ever-present voice in their ear that made them better than most players they faced.

Coach O'Francis' presence as a baseball coach was missed greater than most people ever realized. Harper's "right arm" and his "eyes and ears" were gone. In his unwise and jealous move to regain total control of his ball club, he had killed the one thing that had made his command whole. He alone set everything in motion to have James Patrick O'Francis removed as his assistant. He would play it out as if the administration was totally at fault and hope no one would figure it out. Harper did not realize that James Patrick O'Francis had no desire to become the baseball team's head coach. Jim did not have an overinflated ego and was not power-hungry. Nor was his ego so out of control that he would undercut the head coach. He was happy doing what he did and the position he held.

Getting Personal

Jim and I were on my upper deck and had been talking about some of his more pleasant umpiring experiences, which to me was rather humorous. It had been several years since Jim had been associated with baseball at Honsburg High School. So, I reluctantly brought the question to bear that had been on my list of questions to ask at the proper time.

"Jim, I had heard once that not even Harper could control you. Would you tell me about what he or they meant by control?"

Jim took a very long time to address the question, and for a moment, I thought I had crossed the line in asking such a poignant question.

"Control ... now am I to assume that you mean that I was out of control? Or, on the other hand, that they, whoever *they* may be, could not control me at all? Then there is the meaning of control in itself. Now John, let me think, to have power over, to have direct influence over, and to rule over."

"Well, Jim, either or both, I guess?"

"Then let us talk first about my so-called being out of control. First, let me state I am an emotional coach. So, in many people's eyes, I am out of control.

"Now that is fine if *they*—" He motioned with his fingers out into the open spaces. "—see one of their favorite coaches in whatever sport on TV appear to be "out of control" or, as it is often referred to, "lose it." Now *they* can do that, which is good for the team, fires them up, and gets the team more motivated. Now that is accepted. They love the coach even more than they did before. Yes, there are times in my basketball coaching years when I wish I had had some foresight and had not been so emotional.

"However, the players also see and feel that emotion. And for the most part, the players react positively to the "out-of-control coach." I was never negative in my so-called "out-of-control mode."

"In addition, John, I never got a technical foul while coaching basketball, just for your record. The so-called calm and cool coach does not always get the same reaction from his players. The point of fact is, it is just the opposite. Now John, when it came to baseball that is a different type of game. Some coaches do get emotional. However, I can only remember when I did not control my emotions, and that was after the game had ended. I regretted my actions the instant I reacted to the loss. Which was my fault we lost the game to one of our bitter rivals. There were times I took certain games too personally. I got too involved in the game and forgot I was not a player. I was a coach, so as for Coach O'Francis being "out of control," I only lost my self-control once in all the years of coaching baseball. Does that give you the answer to part one of your question, John?"

"Yes, I do believe I get the idea."

"Now, part two to your question. As for controlling me overall. The job or title of the team's head coach and all of its staff. Well, it is all in the person's perception that holds the top title. It depends on how big his—and I am sure her—ego is. If some staff member is getting too much attention, well, someone has to go, and if that someone is an assistant, oh well ... and the assistant does not have to be a person looking to take over. Remember, I used the term *perception*. Look, the alpha wolf rules. And I am sure you are aware of how that works. It does not make a damn how badly the perceived challenging wolf is damaged. You get rid of them and move on, remaining the alpha wolf. If the team suffers from losing one of its staff, so be it. Ego can be one's Achilles heel in coaching."

In my talks to the players and a few community members, I have often wondered if Harper was not more in tune with the administration and the so-called control issue than the vast majority would ever realize. However, I have learned and pieced together one dominating fact. Harper was quiet, inward, dissembling, and cunning. O'Francis, on the other side of the "pan-cake," was open and free-spirited.

☐

O'Francis had a charisma about him, and all who knew him felt it when they were in his presence.

When he walked onto the field for practice, the players felt it. Their whole attitude would change.

There was something about Coach O'Francis that swept across the park when he entered the confines of a baseball field. Players felt a level of confidence when he was around them. They listened to every word he would say, every gesture. They believed in him. He took them to a higher level, and they had no clue why. I interviewed several players, and they would describe how they felt about O'Francis.

"He just had a walk about him."

"The way he stood or looked, there was something that was surrounding him."

"It was what he would say or how he would say it or something. I really don't know just what it was, but I felt it."

"He just seemed to bring out the very best in me."

"I wanted to do a better job for him. It was as if, ah, it was as if I owed him something. I just seemed to, well ... I just seemed to excel, it was as if things, I mean the game seemed to, well ... I mean I just played better."

"He seemed to understand us."

"He could talk to us on our level, and still, I respected him as a coach. Well, looking back on it now, I just respected him as a man."

"I liked the stories that he told us about his days as a player, some really great stories."

"I don't think that I realized the meaning of some of the things he told me, until I graduated and had to work for a living, what he was saying. Then, it just hit me one day, and I have used his words to get me through some tough times."

"He would take the time to teach us, no matter how long it took. He would be there until we got it."

"He would put down his bat and come running out to my position and show me exactly what he was talking about. Then he would run back to home plate and hit me the ball, and if I did not get exactly what it was he wanted me to do, or the way he felt that it should be done, he would hit me another. He was hard on us, and there were times when I would cuss him under my breath, but now I realize that he was teaching us more than just the game of baseball. Hell, I could tell you several stories about jobs that I have had over the years that Coach's words seemed to come to mind, and things seemed to work out for me."

"I learned more from him about the game of baseball than anyone. And hell, that does not include what he taught me in the classroom."

As I went to each one of these men, I would ask, "What about the head coach, Tim Harper? How did he fit into all of this?"

"*Coach Harper. Well … he was the head coach, I mean officially. But O'Francis, well, he was too, or that is how I looked at it.*"

"*Coach Harper, he was … he just was different. Don't get me wrong. He was a good baseball coach. But he, well … he didn't have whatever it was that Coach O'Francis had. Something, I don't know what it was that was different, but it was something. I really can't put it into words.*"

"*Coach Harper, he was different. He could not communicate with us like Coach O'Francis could. Although he was a good baseball coach, I mean, he knew the game of baseball, but there was something exceptional about O'Francis.*"

"*Harper … wow. Ah, Harper, really never did show any type of feelings … you never really knew if he really cared one way or the other if you lost or won. But, on the other hand, O'Francis, well, he was very emotional … we all knew where he was coming from. Although I might add here, I do not know a*" *player I played with who did not like the way he coached. Oh, and before you ask, yes, that includes his emotion."*

I asked the three I was talking to at the time if he yelled and screamed when they referred to his emotions. *"No, that is not what I meant. He wore his feelings on his sleeve, so to speak. We could tell in his body language, his tone of voice, how he felt. He did not do all that stupid yelling we have seen from other coaches."*

I asked them, "So, together as coaches, how were they?"

"When you put all three of them together, hellll-oooo, man ... I mean, if the umpires had been fair, shit, man. They could have won at least three state championships. Shit. There is no doubt! Hell, you ask anyone who played for them back in those days. They will tell you the same thing."

"Okay, what about Teddy Hurler or 'Humper,' as you have referred to him?"

The former players I talked to praised him with overwhelming accolades, stating he was as good a baseball coach as the official high school coaches. They told me that if he had been given a chance to go to college, he would have been a force in baseball to contend with. He was baseball smart, knew the game inside and out, was quick thinking, and was a good teacher.

I noted that Hurler was always included in any discussions about Honsburg baseball. It was very apparent that the former players had a great deal of respect for Teddy Hurler.

Several told me about various championship games in vivid detail, about how umpires had no honor or honesty and had taken the game away from Harper, O'Francis, and Hurler. The ex-players, now men I talked to, expressed how much it hurt their coaches. They could read Coach O'Francis' face. We could not tell about Harper, but I am sure he was also hurting.

"Teddy, well, even though he tried to hide it, we could tell. But he was a class person, so he, like the rest of us, took the losses, fair or unfair, and went on without a public word."

Several stated that O'Francis showed it more than any one of the three. They described the three as men of honor who played the game with integrity and that if they had been given a fair shot, they would have won games that had been stolen from them, us, with unscrupulous umpires. These players told me that they had played well enough to win but that one or even two umpires could and did turn the game so that the other team would win. They informed me that they had been well prepared. But on more than one occasion, they would have won, but ...

I have watched the man who replaced O'Francis, Andy Ziegler. By all accounts that I have observed and received feedback from players and parents, Ziegler knew the game as well as anyone, but he did not have that, *something* that Coach O'Francis had. By all accounts, he was a very nice man, knowledgeable, an extremely hard worker, and very baseball savvy, but he did not have that mystique. Andy did not have that special touch with the players. In addition, he did not challenge the political power structure or the egotistical, power-controlling head coach.

I have investigated how and why O'Francis was removed, and Ziegler was installed. It seems that the idea came from Tim Harper himself. He alleged that he needed Andy to take over his junior varsity program, which lacked leadership and taught basic skills for the players to be prepared for the next level of play, the varsity.

Harper claimed he had gotten no help from the administration getting a good-quality junior varsity coach for several years. Jim and Harper agreed that *their* (the administration's) plan was to destroy the varsity program by inserting a lesser-qualified person at a lower level. That would ensure that the players they received would be of lesser quality and have a losing season or seasons. If that occurred (which did not happen), the administration would cause dismissal. They could claim they were pressured by the community for a coaching staff to produce winning teams.

The three coaches overcame the shortfalls and produced one winning team after another, despite the efforts of the Damons, Decals, and Finkels and their district school board representative, Barnard Theodoric, of course, all with the approval of the "Fuhrer" (the superintendent).

After lots of investigating, I learned that Harper suggested he and O'Francis pay a visit to Andy at the middle school where he was assigned to teach. They had not seen him in some several years, and only then on the opposite side of the field, as he had at one time been the head baseball coach at Liberty high.

They presented the idea to him. He hesitated and said he would never coach on a varsity level again. He had been the head coach for Liberty High for ten years, but he had crossed the powers of the political machine by not playing whom *they* wanted him to play. Andy lost. They had fired him and had done so in an embarrassing manner, humiliating him in the paper, the only newspaper the county had, located in Liberty, and was solely devoted to emphasizing the Liberty sports programs. Politics always seemed to play a hand in the teachers' and coaches' lives in Reynolds County.

Both Harper and O'Francis knew that Ziegler had the qualities of a good coach, and he had the basic philosophy they had. They knew he had been shafted and felt he would work with them to build a solid junior varsity program. Intellectually, he had it above most other coaches in the area. He knew the game well enough to have given Tim and Jim a run for their money on several occasions. Unfortunately, he had come upon the short end of the stick, having to play against both of their wits. The one thing that O'Francis noted about him when they had faced his teams was that he had not prepared them for special game situations. Of course, Andy did not have any help preparing his teams either. Jim was a devoted advocate. He created game simulations, repeating them daily in practice to where they were second nature to his players. Over the years of interviews, investigating, and research, I have found that had been the secret to the Honsburg baseball program's success. And even though Hurler was not on the list as an assistant coach, he was an intricate part of the game plan.

Jim had great respect for Andy, and he knew the influential political people had done him a great wrong.

The Coffin Nail

James Patrick did not see it coming. He was sold on Harper's idea. So, in his good-hearted effort and loyal to his head coach, he offered Andy a chance to get back into baseball—something Jim knew Andy truly loved. But, during the conversation, Jim could tell that the political powers had all but destroyed Andy's desire to coach again. Something the superintendent of the school system of Reynolds County seemed to marvel at doing. Unless you were "in line."

Andy had been out of the coaching circle for five years and expressed a concern that he may not have it in him to do the job. O'Francis, in his ever-Irish philosophical manner, managed to get him to consider the offer. Harper did little talking to promote his idea, but Jim was used to that and took the lead.

That was only part of the Harper plan. He did not know the type of "pitch" Harper was throwing to use one of Jim's baseball terms. Jim was just not ready for it.

Deep inside the internal workings of Ziegler's baseball soul, there had remained a single ember with a slight glow to it. So, when the now-famous baseball coaching duo and especially the inspirational words of O'Francis had left, it seemed to glow a little brighter.

Little did O'Francis know what he had helped set into motion would seal his fate as a high school baseball coach.

The next concern for the two coaches—would the administration allow Ziegler to coach again? That part of the plan was unclear, and Tim Harper decided that he would have to present the idea to the administration and push it to get Andy into place.

It had been the unrelenting efforts of Jim that had gotten what the baseball team had, not only in material but more especially the facilities, which was still not completed.

I have learned from several sources in and around Honsburg that O'Francis' enthusiasm to obtain the best baseball field in the area and his candid, outspoken character cost him dearly.

Tim presented his plan to Mr. Damon Bales alone. Jim thought it odd that he would do so, as he had never offered any innovative proposal to the administration without O'Francis' presence backing him. But it did not matter to Jim, as he did not like going into Bales' office. Moreover, he had never been in his office for anything positive the entire time Bales had been the administrator of Honsburg High School.

Bale informed Harper that he would consider the matter. Tim thanked him for his time and departed his office. Tim knew what he would do, and he knew that he had planted good seeds and that they would grow and bloom. It just would take a little time.

Bales waited several minutes, got up, walked out to the office lobby, ensured Tim was gone, and went to the phone.

"Reynolds County School Board, may I help you?"

"This is Mr. Bales. I need to speak to Mr. Marshy." A moment passed, and LaMar answered the phone with a big, cheerful, "How are you doing, Damon?"

"LaMar, I have a new plan. I have a way of getting rid of O'Francis."

"You were supposed to get enough on him to fire him two years ago. So, what is the plan?"

"Harper wants Andy Ziegler to coach his junior varsity."

"Why in the hell would you want him added to your staff? Shit, Damon, we got rid of him and are close to getting rid of O'Francis. So, damn it, don't add to the fuckin' problem!"

"Would you go for firing O'Francis from coaching and transferring O'Francis to the middle school? Then we can move Ziegler to the high school and put him in O'Francis' position. Now, LaMar, I think he can be controlled. I do not think he has forgotten what happened to him at Liberty. He will be much easier to deal with than O'Francis. You know that."

There was silence on the line, and Damon continued, "I think this will work. I will need your help on this."

LaMar cleared his throat. "Let me call you back." Then he hung up.

Damon paged Finkel to his office, and in a few minutes, Richard arrived in Bales's office.

Damon smiled with evilness that would have made his dark master very proud. Finally, this new plan that had been dumped into his lap (as he thought, by accident) would work. He felt it in his sinister bones.

Richard entered Bales's office. "Yes, sir, you wanted to see me?"

"I have a plan! First, I will request that O'Francis be transferred to the middle school, and Andy Ziegler be transferred to the high school. Now, here is what I want from you. I want you to tell Andy that he will be replacing O'Francis as the baseball assistant to Tim Harper."

"What if he refuses?"

"He won't. He will have no choice! Once that is done, I want you to tell him he will have the head-coaching job within a year, maybe two at the most."

"How are you going to get rid of Harper?"

Bales waved his hand forward. "Ah, to hell with Harper. With O'Francis out of the way, Harper will come back in line. Tell Andy that Harper has indicated that he is ready to retire and that O'Francis has quit and does not want the head job. Work him and reel him in. Hell, you never know. Harper may fuck up. Although I do not foresee it. He is too conservative. He is more likely to let Andy fuck up, and he will still be behind the curtain. But I also do not see Andy crossing any lines. He has learned a lesson."

"Do you think Andy will do what we ask of him?"

"Ohhh, yes, he will. He will have no choice! Mr. Marshy and I will make sure of that. You leave that to us. You get close to him and use him."

He leaned back in his chair and smiled once again.

The phone rang as Richard was leaving. Bales reached to his left and picked up the phone.

"Mr. Bales," the secretary stated, "Mr. Marshy is on line one."

His voice was one of a happy person. He felt so good; he could have jumped up and clicked his heels together.

"Damon, LaMar here. Come over to my office just as soon as you can get here. I think I have a plan."

That statement made him smile even more, and his blood rushed through his veins at a speed he had not felt in years. To Damon, this was better than sex. His evilness reeked throughout his entire body, and his steps had a quick and bouncy gait to them as he went from the school to his car. No matter how one cuts it, Tim Harper had given Damon Bales the key to destroying James Patrick O'Francis' coaching career and the embarrassment of being demoted to a lower level of education and out of Honsburg High School.

Andy Ziegler did not have a clue as to how evil Damon and Marshy were. He was placed in a position where he was led to believe that he had no choice but to accept the teaching transfer and the coaching position. They made sure that Andy had not contacted Tim Harper before they enacted the transfer and dismissal. As far as Andy knew, when he was in the presence of Bales, Finkel, and Marshy, O'Francis had resigned of his own accord and had requested that he be transferred. Bales laid the story out so smoothly that almost anyone would have believed him.

"Now we are placed in an awful position here, Andy. We need your help."

LaMar never went to any meeting anywhere where he did not have to make some significant statement. He never allowed anyone to outshine him as he chimed in on the conversation.

"Now, Andy, I know you have had a few little differences with the school system in the past. But really, all that is in the past. I know that most of that was brought on by a few radicals around Liberty. But, hell, you know how things can get. Most of us liked you and liked how you ran the baseball program. You know how politics is. But you can help us here. Get yourself back in the baseball groove. You never know, Andy, you may want to be a head coach somewhere again someday. You're a damn good coach, Andy! If I were a principal at a high school, I would want you on my coaching staff."

Two days passed, and Andy called Tim Harper on the phone and informed him of what had happened. Harper listened without speaking as Andy told him the changes that had taken place. Then, Andy asked Harper why Jim had resigned, as he had not indicated that he was ready to give up baseball earlier when they met at the middle school.

For the first time in what had been a one-way conversation, Harper spoke. "He didn't!" Then there was a long silence on the phone.

Andy cleared his throat. "Tim, I was told that ..."

Harper interrupted him. "I have no doubts that is what they told you. But I am telling you that Damon, Finkel, and LaMar did in O'Francis! He had no intentions of quitting baseball! Nor did he want to be transferred! To my knowledge."

"Listen, I am sorry. I didn't know. I mean, what should I do?" Andy Ziegler asked.

"Hell, Andy, there ain't a damn thing you can do! Once they have made a move, it is a done deal."

Tim arrived at the O'Francis home in what appeared to be an ill mood, which was normal for him, as he always seemed to portray the negative. After some bitching about current events, typical for Tim, they sat at the kitchen table, eating dinner with the O'Francis family. He asked if Jim had called Dan Jakes. Jim assured him that he had and that nothing could be done. They had the power to transfer a teacher anytime and anywhere they desired. As to the coaching job, neither the county nor the state considered coaching a job. So, getting fired was not a matter of legal concern by the Teachers Association.

"So, what good is the damn association if they can't help you?" Tim spouted. As if he did not already know.

There was a moment of pause before he replied as O'Francis sat and looked at Tim Harper. His "little voice" was speaking to him. *Harper is dissembling.*

Jim looked at Dawn, standing by the counter across the kitchen. It was as if both had their neurons in their brains lighting up like a Christmas tree, with the same thought. Then Jim spoke slowly with a coldness in his tone of voice.

"I really do not know. It seems that you have to lose everything before the teaching association is willing to come to your legal aid. Hell, then there is no guarantee that they will win. Well, here in this place, at any rate. I damn sure do not have to tell you about that. Christ, they have every judge and political power person in their pocket. Good God Almighty, what a place! I have never seen any place like it!"

Jim stood, indicating it was time for Harper to leave. However, Harper being what he was, remained seated. Jim looked down at him.

"Thanks for coming by. We can talk about this later."

Jim told me in a later conversation, which included that particular day, that just for a few moments, he felt something cold cross through the room. And that when he and Dawn talked after Harper left, she had expressed the same feelings. As I have learned, the two were more than close as husband and wife. There was a spiritual bond between them. He told me that he did not know at the moment what it could be, but in retrospect, we both knew. Then he stated, "Hindsight is fuckin' great, is it not?"

I had to agree.

An Ally

During O'Francis' first semester at his new location of Honsburg Junior High, Bobby Simms assigned Jim a room directly across from a homegrown Honsburg teacher, Mrs. Bernadette Mazo, who taught Science and English. She stood five-three, had short brown hair, and weighed around 115 pounds. Bernadette introduced herself to Jim toward the end of the first six weeks of the school year and offered to help him in any way she could. She had a warm smile and a pleasant face. Jim thanked her and assured her he would call on her if he needed anything, as he knew nothing about the way things worked at the middle school, and he had never taught students at the junior high level.

She did help him and appeared, at any rate, to try to keep him informed on events and procedures that he was not aware of or accustomed to. Now, for Jim, the question was *why* she would help him. He was very aware of the Simms-Bales connection and figured that this being their M.O., she would report anything O'Francis might say that they could use to get rid of him.

After several weeks had passed and several school events had taken place, Bernadette had reminded Jim, keeping him informed, always in a very polite manner, of which he had been very appreciative but remained very skeptical.

Two months passed, and in a rare conversation one afternoon after school hours, meeting Mrs. Mazo in her room as requested, a discussion arose between the two concerning Bobby Simms. Bernadette asked Jim if he had heard anything about Bobby and Ginger having an affair while he was at the high school.

Jim hedged in his answer, but with care, responded, "I can tell you what I saw and what other teachers said. However, keep in mind, what was said by others does not mean that it is true. In addition, Bernadette, what I saw could have been misconstrued, and you can be assured that I did not take what was perceived by me to anyone else in that school. Therefore, I tell you this with great caution to not judge the information as facts. I have learned that not all is what it appears. In addition, I have a great deal of respect for Ginger. She is an outstanding teacher and does care for the students, okay?" He then related the information to her.

After doing so, Bernadette asked, "What do you think?"

"First, I think this conversation is beginning to sound like an inquest. Now, as to what I think of what the gossip grapevine is still spreading, I believe that if one looks at the possibility of an attractive woman with a great deal of intelligence and a not-so-attractive man with absolutely no scruples; if one looks at the type of female she is and the type of male he is, no, I do not think she would lower herself to such a level. As I stated at the beginning of this conversation, perception is everything. It does not make it a fact! In addition, Bernadette, gossip is not facts. This school and this town are full of just that— no offense to your town. I like the town and most people in and around it, despite what the GGV is pandering. It appears to me that the people of your town thrive on GGV."

As Jim was preparing to leave his classroom to go home, the following day, Bobby Simms walked into his assigned room. He closed the door hard and walked briskly to the front of Jim's desk, which struck O'Francis as being somewhat odd, as Simms was usually the one behind the big desk. Only Jim's desk was not quite as plush.

Bobby pulled up a student's desk to the very edge of O'Francis' desk and sat down in it. He was red-faced and with anger in his body language.

"Mr. O'Francis, I would just like to ask you, did you see me and Ginger engaged in any sexual activity?"

O'Francis had been at that point many times before, except at the moment Carl Decal was not accusing him of doing or saying something that did not fit his norm.

"No, sir, I did not, nor have I ever said that you did. So why are you asking me this?"

Bobby Simms continued, "Then to prove anything; you have to see someone first! Am I right?" He slapped his open right hand down on the top of the student's desk.

"I think, Mr. Simms, I have over the many years dealing with you, as well as your sidekick, Carl

Decal, in which I was being accused of statements and or inappropriate activities all being brought to you via hearsay and gossip, I have stated to you that to see or to be present during any type of conversation, or for that matter, activities someone must be present! You do recall me stating that on more than one occasion, correct!"

Bobby Simms reply was, "Good then that will be all of that!"

"All of what, sir?"

"You know what I mean."

"Well, actually, no, I do not." O'Francis' voice became firmer and with a coldness to it.

"I mean any conversations to any other teacher in this school about me or anyone else."

Jim broke a slight smile. "Well, sir, just let me say this. I do not control what others may or may not say. As for myself, I am not sure where you might have gotten the idea that I was engaged in any nefarious conversation concerning you and or Ginger. I think you and I have been in this position many times in our storied past, except I was the one on the receiving end of the accusations and gossip. "The *have you heard, did you know*, and so on." But, in addition, Mr. Simms—" As James Patrick's voice became slightly more elevated, his facial expression became harder. "—I recall quite clearly, and you seemed to always agree with the people bringing you the accusations which directly concerned me!"

Simms sat for a moment looking at O'Francis, then got up, placed the desk back where he had gotten it, and began to walk toward the door.

O'Francis waited until he just about reached the door. "Mr. Simms," Jim said, "As for being accused of an event or events that may or may not have occurred in your past, I will tell you this. I personally do not care one way or the other. It did not affect my family or me. So, again, just make myself clear in this conversation, I have not made any false accusations about you or anyone else in this community in the past or presently! If I tell someone of some event or occurrence that reflects someone personally, it is checked out beforehand and is factual. Jim's voice became more pronounced. "I have neither in the past nor presently accepted hearsay from others as fact! Now, as we stand here facing each other once again with accusations of some alleged infidelities of type out of the professed Honsburg community's alleged norms, with a bit of a different twist to it all, you can be assured of one thing. I have and had the utmost respect for Ginger."

Then after a slight pause, Jim continued. "I will not be a part of any conversation in the confines of this educational institution about any past alleged occurrences that may have involved you personally. You have my word. That, I think you know. My word is bond. It is a done deal if I tell you I will or will not do something. Now, Mr. Simms, how about you giving me the same courtesy for once?"

Simms stood across the room, looking at Mr. O'Francis, saying nothing. Jim spoke firmly. "Sir, which is more than I can say has taken place in my life while living in your community, according to sources that would include you, sir. You now have my word. Do I have yours?"

Simms stood across the room with a stark expression on his face. Then, before he could turn, Jim shot one more volley across his bow, with an even more deadly tone in his voice. "I do not deal in character assassination."

Simms turned boldly, took two steps to the door, and opened it harshly, exiting the room, leaving the door open.

Jim scooted his chair back a bit, slowly sat down, and placed his feet up on the edge of his shabby-looking desk. His hands cupped together, his two index fingers gently bouncing back and forth off his lips as he sat pondering. It *seems that my conversation with Bernadette may have struck a nerve. The facts in the matter are that I did not state that any of it was true. I thought I had made myself clear. Oh well, it is what it is. He also did not give me his word that he would not repeat gossip related to me, so much for honor on his part. So, what is new in my world? Now the question begs to be asked, where did he get his information?*

Jim spoke aloud softly to no one in his presence. "Mr. Martin was directly across the hall, and Bernadette's classroom door was open when we were talking. So he could have easily heard the conversation, as our voices would carry in an empty classroom.

"Or another possibility is Bobby could have listened in over the intercom. He could have seen me go into Bernadette's room. Annie Alderman, who had stopped by momentarily and then left, was the only other person to come into the room or the area. She could have heard us talking. Nah, Annie did not fit the typical gossip lounge teacher. I just do not know. Oh well... I sure cannot expect anything better! Just have to deal with it—my mistake. I have to get a job somewhere else. This place will kill me if I do not. What a hellhole. There is not another human being on earth that would believe all this shit!"

As Jim gathered his briefcase and exited his classroom, He mentally talked to himself. *There is one fact that all these son-of-bitches do not realize. I have sources far beyond their little "pond-minds" could comprehend! Time is on my side when it comes to that alternative!* Jim smiled as he exited the building and walked to his car.

Patrick's Day Off

Jim went about his job as if nothing ever happened, adapting and hoping to overcome his new world of teaching pre-high school students. Bobby became friendlier and more pleasant with him as the year progressed. Bernadette would become close friends and a proven ally to O'Francis when it appeared that the cards were stacked against him in the years to come, leaving James Patrick to believe that it was not Bernadette who had informed Bobby of their conversation.

☿

Patrick was having problems with his science teacher, Fred Martin. Jim tried to be professional, as he had to work with Fred. However, he would hear the women teachers who worked in his section of the building talk about Fred in a manner that would have chilled hell with their words. Now, O'Francis did not know the man and couldn't have cared less about how the women felt, as long as he treated his son fairly.

As he arrived home, Dawn had a troubled look on her face. "Bobby Simms called today."

"What did he want?"

"Patrick got in trouble in Mr. Martin's class."

"For what?"

"Well, according to Patrick, Mr. Martin yelled at him for answering a question incorrectly. And it was not the first time he had done so."

"Okay."

"Well, Patrick called him a damn faggot, and Mr. Martin sent him to the office."

"He did not say anything to me on the way home."

"Well, at any rate, Bobby told me that he was suspending him for one day."

Jim called Patrick into the kitchen and had him explain what happened to him in his science class.

The O'Francis family accepted the punishment and tried to get along, encouraging Patrick to work hard with his studies, and it would work out in the long haul. He would face many types of obstacles throughout his life, and he would have to learn to deal with each of them; he would learn from the one before. But for their thirteen-year-old son, it was tough to understand why a teacher was being unfair to him and treating him harshly in class, embarrassing him in front of his classmates.

Fred copped an attitude toward Patrick, and his grades dropped from B's to D's to F's, which concerned Dawn and Jim, as Martin's science class began to affect his other classes, even his father's history class. Patrick was getting to the point that he hated school. It became an everyday event between Fred Martin and Patrick O'Francis. Patrick had history after his science class and would come into his father's class stressed out and upset. It would take him half the period before he would settle down to the point that he could gain any knowledge about history.

This Jim had noticed in several other students as well. From time to time, Jim reported his concerns to Mr. Simms. For example, Jim told Simms that there appeared to be a problem in Fred Martin's class with certain students.

On Patrick's day off, he rode an eighteen-ton tri-axle rock truck with Peter Henry Stacy, who went back to truck driving after he had lost his job as a police officer because of the political machine.

New sheriff, different political party, new deputies, and if you were not one of the "good ole boys," you look for a new job. It did not make a royal rat's ass how much experience you had or how good a law-enforcement person you were. You're out, cold, cut, and dried!

Of course, the new "law in the county" was not qualified, nor would they have the leadership of a William Peng. The ethics and honor would also go with Peng. But William had never walked to the drumbeat of the political powers. He walked to the beat of *his* drum, and that was, of course, why he did not last more than one term in office as the Reynolds County sheriff.

Patrick's day with Peter was delightful, as Peter picked him up at 5:00 a.m. and worked until 5:00 p.m. For a thirteen-year-old, that was a full day. Peter was one of a very few people in the area who had not jumped on the bandwagon of accusing O'Francis of any wrongdoing and had not believed all the gossip that had floated through the vast network of sewer lines in the county community. Nevertheless, Peter remained a true friend to the O'Francis family and would drop in from time to time for a brief visit and a cup of coffee.

The following six weeks, Jim made arrangements with Bobby Simms to meet with Fred Martin after his regular working hours. He informed Simms that he would be a parent, not a colleague. Jim also requested that Mr. Simms be present for the parent-teacher conference. However, Jim was not a very happy camper, as he took it personally when some adult attacked his sons.

The meeting was set for 3:45 p.m. Bobby had informed Mr. Martin that Mr. O'Francis would be meeting him as a parent, and when Simms confirmed the appointment, Simms indicated that Fred did not have any problem with the meeting.

At three forty-five, James Patrick entered Fred Martin's room.

"Afternoon Mr. Martin."

"Afternoon," Martin replied.

Bobby Simms was not present, and Jim waited for five minutes before addressing Fred Martin about his son. Jim did not know why Simms was late. His thoughts were that he was setting him up for something so he could fire him. Bobby knew how he felt about his sons and knew that he would not let anything happen to them. James O'Francis had warned Bobby Simms that his sons were never to be stuck with a "paddle" (a piece of wood, a weapon.) I told him face to face if it happened, he would do the same to the person who stuck his sons.

Jim figured Simms thought he would lose it and take Fred out, leaving him no choice but to recommend being dismissed. That, Jim, did not intend to happen. He had been through too much to lose control. He would handle the matter in a controlled manner. If Fred did not cooperate, he would walk away.

"Fred, what seems to be the problem between my son and you?" Jim sat in one of the front-row students' desks. Fred chose to stand at the taller black-topped science table located directly in the front of the room, which was Mr. Martin's desk.

"I didn't know that we had a problem."

"Oh, I see. Well, okay, good. Then could you tell me why Patrick's grades have dropped from B's to F's?"

"He's not doing the work."

"Well, Fred, what about this past six weeks? I mean, look... he did a project, and what was his grade on that? It was a rather large project, and he spent a lot of time on it. Also, what of the test grades did he receive these six weeks? What were they? I have asked him to bring home each test paper to go back over the ones he may have missed. However, he tells me that you have not returned any of his test papers. May I see them or the grades that he received for them?"

Fred had taken a seat a few feet from Jim by that point in the conversation.

"I don't know what I have done with his test papers."

"Well, fine. Let's look at Patrick's grades in your grade book."

"Why?" Martin asked firmly.

"I beg your pardon?" Jim asked.

"I said why? Why do you need to see your son's grades?"

"Well, Fred, it is customary to show a parent their child's grades and what tests they have taken and what they made on each of the tests. Do you not do that with other parents? He was not absent a single day, so he had to have taken all the tests you had scheduled for the six weeks."

O'Francis took out his pen, went to his briefcase, and got out a notepad.

"What do you think you are doing?" Martin asked.

"I am going to copy each test, date, and grade down. That is what I am doing, Fred." Jim looked up at Fred as he suddenly jumped out of the student's desk.

"I don't have to put up with this!" Out of no apparent provocation, he had taken offense and become angry.

"Look, Fred." Jim rose to face him. "I am here as a parent with concerns for my son. I expect you to cooperate with me. I am not here to attack you in any way. Hell, man, I have been through this probably a hundred times. I am not your enemy. All I want is to get a grip on my son's progress and find out what is going on. Come on, how about a little cooperation here, okay?"

"I ain't saying nothing else!"

"So you are refusing to work with me on this? Is that what you are telling me, Fred?"

He turned and angrily left the room, leaving Jim standing next to the students' desks. Jim sat back down and waited. Five minutes passed, and Bobby Simms came in.

"Where is Mr. Martin?" He asked.

"Well, Mr. Simms, he has left the room. I presumed that you would have seen him in the hall or that he went to your office."

"Have you all started yet?"

"Yes, sir, that we have." Bobby Simms looked puzzled and pulled up a desk just to Jim's right.

"Well, is he coming back, or is the meeting over? I mean, did you two get everything worked out okay?"

"Well, not really, Mr. Simms. I would have appreciated it if you had been here when we started. I do believe you would have found it to be fascinating."

"What does that mean?"

"As a parent, and looking at it from a teacher's point of view, I have never treated any parent in the manner I have just been treated. And if I had, you and any of my previous bosses would have most likely had legitimate grounds to take me in front of the school superintendent and board. I am talking about legitimate grounds, not the ones that have been used in the past. Now, as a parent, I am filing with you right now," Jim said as he pointed his right index finger toward the desktop, "an official complaint against Mr. Fred Martin. I would also like you to find out why Mr. Martin is harassing my son. I expect it to stop!"

At that moment, Fred Martin walked back into the room and instantly went off like a Roman candle. He froze three feet into the room.

"By God, I ain't meeting with him in here!" He pointed his finger toward Bobby Simms.

"Fred," Jim said with concern, "let's—"

He interrupted Jim. "I told you I ain't saying nothing in front of him! Why is he in here anyway?"

"Fred, calm down. He is the principal, or have you forgotten? I asked him to stop by, and it is customary to meet with a parent when a student has a problem. I mean, what is the problem?"

"No, no, no, he goes, or I go!"

"No, now Fred, look ... let's iron this out today, let's you and me..."

"Hell no, not as long as *he* is in here!" He turned and walked out again, leaving Jim and Simms looking at each other.

In a calm voice, O'Francis spoke. "Well, Mr. Simms, I would call that a gross case of insubordination. If I had done just that—no, let me rephrase that. Anywhere near that to you... oh well, I did not, would never, and have never treated a parent anywhere near the way I have just been treated."

Mr. Simms sat, saying nothing.

"So, Mr. Simms, I guess that means we will meet in your office, officially, with my wife present. I want to meet Friday at 0900 hours. I will be taking the day off as I will be here as a parent. Sir, I will put in for a personal leave day."

Jim got up first, leaving Simms sitting at the student's desk as he walked out of the room and went home to Dawn and Patrick. He informed her of what had taken place.

Friday arrived, and the O'Francis parents were at the school at 8:55 a.m. and were escorted into Mr. Simms's office. In a short time, Mr. Simms entered with Mr. Martin. For Jim, it was an odd feeling being on the flip side of the pancake. He was hoping that he would not have to say anything and that Dawn would do all the talking. But Fred being Fred and having an attitude toward them and their son did not work out as Jim hoped. As much as he hated to, he finally stepped into the conversation when Fred continued to verbally attack Dawn and Patrick, referring to his son as someone he would expect to find on the street corner in leathers and chains and dealing drugs. Mr. Simms seemed to have no control over Mr. Martin, and when Fred refused to answer Dawn's questions about her son's grades for the fourth time, Jim spoke.

"Mr. Martin, you are making more out of this than needs to be. We want to clear this matter up here in Mr. Simms's office, and we can proceed with just a little cooperation."

Fred Martin laughed at both of them.

"Look, Mr. Martin, if you do not want to clear this up here, we can take it to the superintendent. Then, after that, it is up to you."

"You can take it to whoever you want! I don't have to clear up anything!" He got up, opened the door, and walked out.

"Mr. Simms, Fred has given us no choice but to go to the superintendent. So, now I have followed all the guidelines and chain of command."

"Well, Mr. and Mrs. O'Francis, I guess you will just have to do what you think is best."

Then Dawn spoke as Jim rose from his chair. "We are doing what is best for our son. I want him out of his classroom today."

"Now, Mrs. O'Francis, you know I can't do that."

"Excuse me! You did not seem to have a problem doing it with students in my husband's classes over the years! You and every other damn principal he has had to work for! Yes, you can! And I do not want Patrick to spend another day in *Mr. Martin's* room!"

"Mr. O'Francis."

"No, Mr. Simms, this time, Mr. Martin is wrong, and he has not been treating Patrick fairly. Regrettably, it affects Patrick's grades, and we cannot allow that. I do not want my son to have to go to that class another day."

The O'Francis parents left Simms's office and went straight to the superintendent.

After a thirty-minute conversation with the superintendent, where Dawn finally became emotional, Jim could see that LaMar enjoyed every minute of it. Jim watched LaMar as Dawn explained the problem to him. His thoughts flashed through his mind like a lightning bolt. *He couldn't care less. He has the political mannerisms down to a fine art. He should have been a professional politician, showing the mother genuine concern and making that little caring comment.*

"Now, Mrs. O'Francis, I care about the welfare of all the students in our system, and if there is something wrong, I will look into it and correct any wrong. I like old Patrick. Bet he is a lot like his dad."

Then a big laugh rolled out of his overly loud mouth.

Again Jim's mind raced at an accelerated speed.

He is just making Dawn think something will be done to justify the wrong being done. And I caught that demeaning comment that he is just like his dad. But, of course, if it was anyone else, and it was O'Francis on the hot seat, he would do something! How easy would it be for me to eliminate him right here? God, if I only could and walk away.

LaMar interrupted Jim's thoughts. "Mr. O'Francis, so you have tried to come to, let's say, terms with Mr. Martin?"

Jim smiled. "That is correct." Then, a momentary pause. LaMar expected some type of follow-up statement. It did not come.

"Ahhh, is there anything else you want to say?" LaMar asked.

"No," Jim responded coldly.

Jim knew there would be no investigation into the matter, and nothing would be done to help them or their son. The O'Francis family could expect no satisfaction from the Reynolds County School System.

Patrick did have to attend Mr. Martin's class, but he would not have to do any work for the remainder of the year. Therefore, he would receive a D for the remaining six weeks and a D for the year.

Jim and Dawn were angry, as they knew he would not be prepared for his high school science classes, making it harder for him in the upper grades. But it would give the people connected to the overall conspiracy an opportunity to strike again at Jim through his son by giving him a bad grade in his course load and claiming that he just could not do the work.

Jim would once again realize that he had all the cards stacked against him, which made him much more bitter, and the hatred grew stronger and stronger.

The stress mounted on him as he visualized the assassination of all involved. He fought to control his innermost desires to relieve the painful hate he was going through. But once again, he was brought to the forefront of the reality that he was not part of the political machine and the game he was in. A game he had no interest in.

The Players

It was spring, and baseball was in the air. Jim was hurting, as he was not on the field coaching the sport he so dearly loved. He had been scheduled his first umpiring game and given the plate to call. After all the years of coaching, he found himself wearing the blue shirt. It had been many years since he had called an official game, and he was a bit tight, as he knew how important each pitch was to the young men on the mound.

He had invested in a top-quality set of equipment: two pairs of charcoal slacks and two blue shirts; one pair of plate shoes and a pair of base shoes; two caps, one to be used for the bases and one with the shorter bill for the plate, allowing for his mask to fit over it.

His shoes had a high-gloss shine, his gig line was straight. He placed a chew of beechnut in his right cheek. Then he stepped to the plate, turned his back to the pitcher, took his plate broom out of his right pouch, bent over, and cleaned home plate off. Finally, he straightened up, looked at the catcher, who was standing in his catcher's box behind the plate, Jim asked, "Are you ready to play ball?"

A junior in high school, the catcher held his mask in his right hand, smiled, and replied, "Yes, sir."

Jim smiled. "Then let's get this game going. It sure doesn't work without us."

He then turned back to the pitcher and stated, "Play ball!" He pulled his tan-leathered padded mask over his face and stepped behind the catcher as the first batter positioned himself in the batter's box.

He was very comfortable behind home plate, as he had been a catcher himself, and enjoyed the role of chief umpire. Over the next six years, he would be known among coaches as a very fair and impartial umpire. Some of them he had faced as a coach, although the coaches often would not agree with his calls, be it a base ump or a plate umpire. He was good at his job, and there was never a game that he did not do his best to improve over the last game he called. He knew the game and knew the rules. Jim did his best to read the rulebook and the casebook as many times as possible. He knew that he would never reach 100 percent perfection but intended to try.

It bothered him when he missed a call. He would replay it over and over in his mind so as not to make the same mistake again. The one quality he had over many umpires he had known as a coach and as a colleague, whether he liked the coach or not, was that he never made a call in malice to get back at any coach. He knew that the players were playing the game, not the coaches, and he would call them as he saw them.

Coaches requested Jim to call many of their games. Especially the games that would determine a conference championship.

Once again, the Damon-Finkel factor attempted to discredit O'Francis. On the orders of Damon, Finkel called the commissioner of baseball after receiving a list of umpires who would be used for the season. Richard requested that O'Francis not be used for any of the Honsburg games, at home or away. Finkel did not know most of the coaches, and 90 percent of all the umpires in the umpiring association were very much aware of the way Jim O'Francis had been treated over the years. But when Richard asked Ed Lowe if he knew anything about O'Francis and with a fabricated *no* for a reply, Richard proceeded to assassinate Jim verbally.

Ed scheduled a game the second week of the season to work with Jim and evaluate him personally. He knew his quality as a coach over many years of seeing him operate. Ed calculated that if he were anywhere close to as good at umpiring as a coach, he would be one of the best the association had.

Outside of the confines of the playing field, in their pregame prep, Ed told Jim of the conversation with Jim's nemesis, Richard Finkel.

"So, what are you going to do, Ed?" Jim asked.

"I am going to schedule you like I do any other umpire. Now, do you want to call any of the Honsburg games? I mean, it is no real problem for me. Neither Richard Finkel nor Damon Bales controls this organization, nor will they ever as long as I am the commissioner."

"Well, Ed, I do not think that the other coaches would appreciate me calling Honsburg's games when they had to face Tim and me last year as coaches. Now, do not read me wrong. I still would call them as

I see them. The point of fact is, Tim would most likely give me a harder time than any of the other coaches ever would. He never did like my low strike zone when I would call during our practices. But I would not feel comfortable calling a Honsburg game. I am too close to the players. As far as the coach goes, well...so, for all of Richard's efforts to discredit me, it went for nil. Let it go. Let him and the rest of the assholes ... no, let me correct myself. An asshole does have a purpose in life. These people have no positive, productive purpose. They really should be exterminated. These people are a disease in our society and should be eliminated. Sorry, Ed, it is just that I have a lot of anger in me."

"Hell, you don't have to explain a damn thing to me. Shit, I am surprised that you haven't put one of the bastards in the hospital or the grave already with as much as you have gone through. Jim, the baseball community, is well aware of what has gone on in the baseball program at Honsburg. Word gets around. Every one of us knows what has gone on. So, you owe me no apology whatsoever. And I think you will find that most, if not all, the other umpires feel the same way. I have never heard one that did not like to come

to yours and Tim's place to call a game. I don't think—
I am not real sure about this, but I don't think any of
us has ever had a confrontation with either one of you
for ... how many years?"

"Tim and I were together for ten years. And you
are very most correct. We have never had a problem
with any umpire. Now that does not mean we liked
the calls all the time, and I know you are very much
aware of some of the games we have been fucked on!
However, those games most likely cost us at least one
state title, and I am not sure we could have won two
more. And I mean that I really do believe that!"

"Oh, yes, I am very much aware of the games
that you have been screwed on! But there is one thing
that can never be taken away from you two. You were
a class act, no matter what the outcome was. And that
goes for your players as well. There are not a lot of
teams that I can say that about."

"All a player is, that is, with his actions on and
around the game, reflects the coaches. I thank you for
the kind words," Jim stated as they walked onto the
field to start the game.

Michael was in his second semester of college, as was his close friend Stacy Cross. Both had struggled as freshmen because of the lack of high school preparation. But that did not surprise Jim, as he had said many times that, for the most part, the teachers at the school were a joke. There were a few exceptions, maybe five or six, but no more. He was proud to be one of those who prepared the students. The courses these few taught their students that did go off to higher education, did very well, and often came back to thank Jim and a few of the actual teachers who had prepared them for college.

Dawn had been unable to get a job in the area, and the money to run their household was again depleted at the end of each month. If he could make a thousand dollars umpiring, it would keep them out of the red. Jim stayed depressed most of the time because he could not give Michael any spending money. Finally, he told Dawn that he would be going to Detroit to get a summer job and stay with Dennis and Theresa.

In one of his trips to his attorney, Holly suggested that Jim see a psychoanalyst that it might help him with his stress, and after some thought, he decided to do so. Holly did not know and couldn't have cared less because the money was not there for any doctor, mental or physical. He had to borrow the money from his mother-in-law to pay for Holly's services.

Of course, it was not the first time Jim sought psychotherapy and most likely would not be the last. However, he had not found any relief from any one of them over the years. So, Dawn and Jim sat down and did their calculations about how to stretch the dollar just a little more for at least a brief period.

He started his mental therapy in March of that year and had to go once a week. He frequently felt that he was wasting his time and valued money but did what had been advised. He thought that maybe it would help keep him balanced enough not to do something stupid.

Self-Discipline

It was the last six weeks of school, and even though the umpiring job had turned out to be a success, and the extra money had exceeded expectations, the coffer had little left at the end of each month.

The year had gone without any significant allegations of O'Francis' wrongdoings. Jim had been thankful for it. However, during the last few weeks of the school year, he had difficulty out of one of his seventh graders. Kent Wilfred had interrupted his lectures on more than one occasion, and it seemed that he could not reach the boy, no matter what he did. The administration did not want to deal with him because of his mother, whose "bubble" did not come close to being between the lines. So they just threw him back at Jim. However, Jim noted that if one of the female teachers sent Kent to the office, they handled the matter and sent him home for several days on more than one occasion.

It was not a particularly bad day for O'Francis, but Kent's outburst of "hee-haw, jackass" style of laughter during a lecture on Vietnam did not sit well with O'Francis.

He stopped in the middle of his lecture and stated, "Kent, if you continue to act and sound like a jackass in my class, I will remove you for the remainder of the year! *Do you understand me?*" His voice had become very direct, harsh, and profound.

The following day, Jim entered his room, running three minutes late, as he had gone to the restroom to empty a bladder full of coffee, and walked to his podium.

"Okay ...let me see ... fourth period ...okay, where were we? Someone give me a brief breakdown of yesterday's lecture."

Usually, several students tried to talk at once. He had to remind them that only one was to speak at a time, trying to teach them the manners of not talking over one another, which Jim hated and noticed that people in general did. More women than men, except media reporters and commentators, and then gender did not matter. They all were rude. However, no one spoke that day, and there was total silence in the room. He looked up and scanned the room as it hit him that something was not just right in his now-famous "Think Tank," as it had been called for many years on the high school level and now on the junior high level. It had not registered with him that no one had been talking as he entered the room. That was not normal. Except when there was a guest in the room, the rule was that if there was a guest or a colleague or principal, no one spoke out of order. He admired his students for adhering to the rules.

As he scanned the room, there was a woman he did not recognize in the back of the room. He had not scheduled any parent conferences, which would have been during his morning break, and none had any parent asked to sit in on his class that day, which on occasion a parent did, and Jim allowed it.

Jim had informed the administration that he was a professional and intended to be treated as such. Simms had mildly objected to the conversation about just sending a parent to his room without prior notification. Jim was not sure whether he had been playing the devil's advocate or not but had responded.

"Do you walk into a doctor's office and demand to see your physician? No, I do not think so. Do you walk into your lawyer's office and demand to see your attorney? No, again, I do not think so. Try walking into your congressmen's office and demanding to see him. I am a professional, and I will be treated like one. If someone would like to see me, they can make an appointment, and I will be more than glad to see them if I do not have something of importance scheduled at the time."

Simms had agreed that anyone who just stopped by to see him for whatever reason would first have to contact him and get his approval before allowing them to come to Jim's room.

James Patrick walked to within a few feet of the woman. "Madam, may I help you?"

"May I help you, madam," came the sneering comeback. "Just who the fuck do you think you are?"

Jim cut her off quickly. "Look ... I do not know who you are, but you will have to leave my room. I have a class to conduct!"

"Shit! I ain't going anywhere, *Mr. O'Francis!*" she stated in a challenging, drawn-out manner.

O'Francis turned to look directly at one of the female students sitting close to the door.

"Barbara, would you please go to the office and ask Mr. Simms to come to my room? I have a problem."

She was up and gone in a flash, as everyone saw a dangerous situation.

The woman harshly responded, "You have a God damn problem, all right. You're going to think fucking problem when I get done with you!"

"Who are you?" Jim inquired.

"I am Kent Wilfred's mother, and I... "

Once again, Jim cut her off.

"Will you please step outside of my room Mrs. Wilfred?" He indicated with his left arm and hand to the direction of the door.

Mrs. Wilfred got up out of the student's desk and violently shoved it to her right, colliding with the student to her right.

"You're a piece of shit!" So stating as she glared at O'Francis, passing him, and walked to the door in a manner that would indicate a woman angry and emotionally distraught.

Kent was sitting in his assigned seat at the other side of the room, smiling as Jim followed Mrs. Wilfred out the door, closing it behind him. His primary concern was to get her away from the students. He had been told that she was not at all stable, and he did understand that part. On the other hand, he was well aware that an unstable person without self-discipline was a threat to all in their presence. Several students looked back at Kent when the door closed.

"Hey, don't look at me like that," Kent stated. "Shit, he brought it on, and my mother will kick his ass!" Several boys laughed lightly.

"Sure, Kent, I can just see that!"

"Yeah, well, my dad will bury his ass! He ain't all that bad! Hell, my dad will blow his ass away! He's just a damn teacher."

Patrick finally turned in his seat and boldly defended his father from across the room.

"You know, Kent, you and your whole damn family, are nothing but trash!"

"Look, you little fat piece of shit, I'll come up there and beat your ass!"

Since the size difference between the two was well in favor of Kent, who was, for a thirteen-year-old, six-foot-one, and two hundred–plus pounds, and Patrick, who at thirteen, five-foot-six and 160 pounds, it would have been Patrick's doomsday. However, being the O'Francis he was, and even though fearing the overbearing giant sitting in the back of the room, all the junior high students were afraid of, Patrick called his bluff, knowing he would get his face smashed in. However, his friend Curt, who was about the same size as Patrick and had a passive demeanor, to a point, and who would forever remain his friend, had Patrick's back. It would have most likely taken both of them to have handled Kent.

Patrick challenged the brute.

"Well, I don't see anyone stopping you. But, of course, Mommy is just outside the door. Maybe you can call on her!"

The boys in the room were excited. A fight was about to take place, and for all boys in junior high school, a fight was something to behold. Now, Curt was not much on the physical aspect of resolving a dispute. He was more intellectual, and diplomacy was the better part of valor. However, being a country boy and choosing between trying to talk to an idiot and coming to the aid of his friend, Curt would opt for the physical part of resolving the matter. Jim could hear voices raised in the room, reopened the door, and looked throughout the room. He did not have to speak. Silence swept over the room like a black death cloud.

Mr. Simms and Mr. Cosworth, his assistant, were coming down the hallway in a manner that indicated an emergency. Barbara was only thirty feet in front of them, approaching the door to the classroom, and Jim let her in and then closed the door.

Jim politely and calmly stated, "Mr. Simms, I would like for you to escort Mrs. Wilfred away from my classroom, please."

"I have told you, you sonofabitch, that I ain't going nowhere!" She placed her hand on the doorknob, shifted her hips to her right. "You think you are some kind of real tough guy! I have heard all about you, and I ain't afraid of you! My husband was in the army too! He *will* put you in the hospital or bury you here or downtown!"

Mr. Simms interrupted her.

"Mrs. Wilfred, please come with me to the office, and let's see if we can clear up whatever it is that is bothering you."

"This ... *this*," as she looked at Jim, "is what is bothering me! He'll not talk to my boy like he did and get away with it!"

"Mrs. Wilfred, I don't know what you are talking about, but ..."

"Oh, I am sure you don't! *I know how you all stick together up here!* You all pick on Kent all the time, and I am damn fed up with it, and I intend to do something about it here and now!"

Jim reached for the doorknob with his right hand.

"Oh no, you don't! Don't you ... you even think about it, mister! I'll slap the hell out you, you sonofabitch!"

O'Francis took a deep breath, and in the most polite voice and tone he could, said, "Please, Mrs. Wilfred. I really do not think you want any problems here today. Now, if you would please just go with Mr. Simms and Mr. Cosworth, I am sure they will hear your complaint, and we will resolve the matter."

O'Francis looked at his administrators.

"Sirs, I am asking you to allow me to return to my class. Enough is enough, and I am losing patience real fast."

Neither man would step closer than six feet— the exact position they had come to when arriving at O'Francis' room.

"Mrs. Wilfred, if you would just come with me, please."

Mr. Simms spoke as calmly as he could. Jim knew that both administrators had more than one encounter with her, none being delightful.

"I will allow you to tell me all about whatever bothers you. I promise you we will take care of the matter."

O'Francis reached for the door, and Mrs. Wilfred slapped his hand away, glaring at him.

"Yeah, sure! I'm not through with you!" Then, her face drawn with anger, pointing her finger at Jim, she turned toward Bobby and Darrel and walked down the hallway. Getting some thirty feet away, she turned just as Jim opened the door, pointing her finger at him.

"You're dead! You're dead, you sonofabitch!"

After Jim's sixth-period class had ended, Mr. Cosworth came to his room five minutes into the last class of the day and informed him that Mr. Simms wanted him in the office and that he would stay with his class. Jim looked at Darrel with concern on his face.

"I take it that things did not go well?"

"Ahhh, no. Not at all! But that is normal for her!"

O'Francis pecked on Mr. Simms's office door.

"Come in." Mr. Simms said, his voice indicating that he was nervous. Jim entered. Two chairs were against the wall to the left of the door as he entered, facing Simms' desk. One chair was to the right of the door against the wall. Mrs. Wilfred was sitting in the far chair. Jim closed the door and sat in the one on Simms's left.

"Mr. O'Francis, Mrs. Wilfred stated that you called her son a jackass in front of the entire class. Is that true?"

"Yes," O'Francis responded.

Mrs. Wilfred jumped on that instantly. Her voice was raised, and her face filled with anger.

"My son doesn't use that kind of language, nor do we around him! Now, I want something done about him now!"

Mr. Simms looked at Jim. "Ahhh, Mr. O'Francis, do you want to say anything?"

"Yes, I do." He explained why he chose to use the terms he did, which brought on a five-minute verbalizing assault, charging Jim with cussing her little boy. Jim was well aware of Kent's afterschool curriculum, lying out on the street corner with drug hustlers at all hours of the night. Jim uncrossed his left leg.

"Sir, May I be excused? I do not think we will resolve anything here and now."

Mrs. Wilfred quickly spoke. "You're right. You will apologize to my little boy and me!"

Jim did not wait for Simms to excuse him. Instead, he turned and walked out of the office.

☿

Within a week of Mrs. Wilfred's display of ignorance, Mr. Marshy sent his leading SS people to Honsburg Middle to investigate the events and Jim.

Again Dan was called to come to the assistance of James Patrick O'Francis, which irritated LaMar to the point of violent vernacular verbalization of him. Once in a display of his true self, after losing to Dan in another of his attacks on O'Francis, he stated he would like to kill Dan Jakes. But like O'Francis, Dan had faced actual death many times, and unlike Marshy, who had dodged the draft during the Vietnam conflict and became a basic coward, he was no match for either Dan or Jim, on or off the "playing field."

Marshy could do him harm behind the scenes— acts of sabotage and character assassination, keeping the pressure on in hopes that Jim would break, using the ignorance of some of Jim's colleagues and his principals. They were controlled by the money Marshy made sure they received in salaries and other perks. Especially his very close office staff.

In the end, James Patrick would have to face the reality of the power of his conspirators. He would be presented with a statement by Simms that informed him that any future complaints concerning the same issues would result in severe disciplinary action taken against him. Bobby Simms requested that he sign the document, but O'Francis refused, informing him that he was not guilty of cussing anyone and had never directly cursed a student in his career. Nevertheless, Simms told him a copy would be placed in his file.

"Well, Mr. Simms, that being the case, I will have Mr. Jakes respond to your document with a letter denouncing any wrongdoing I am charged with."

James Patrick paused momentarily before walking out of the Simms office.

"Mr. Simms ... if I had been one of the boys or a split-tail, we would not be having this conversation!" He then turned and exited the office.

☿

Fate Being Their Guide

It was June, and Jim was trying to repair his water heater, as they had no extra money to get a much-needed new one. Dawn walked into the laundry room.

"I will call Dennis after I finish here and leave for Detroit Saturday."

She just stood looking at her beloved soulmate for a good five minutes.

"I saw a help wanted sign in the video store downtown. I think I will apply for the job. What do you think?"

"Well, if you can get the job, it would save me from leaving you all alone for the summer. How much does it pay?"

"I'm not sure. I need to call."

"You got the number?" Jim asked.

"Yes, their main office is in Harriette."

He struggled with his repairs and said, "Damn, I hate this damn thing! Fuck, nothing works anymore!"

Sitting back on the concrete floor, he pushed himself against the wall and relit his cigar, which he had chewed half away. Then, finally, he looked up at his wife, who was still standing in the doorway, with a look that said, *I wish I could make it all better.*

"Look, we have to do something. Call them now; see if they will give you an interview."

So Dawn went to the phone and made the call, and to both of their surprise, they asked if she could come for an interview the next day.

They arrived in Harriette ten minutes before her interview. Both had discussed her getting a job and what it would mean during the forty-five-minute trip it took to get to Harriette, and both kept a positive approach to the job possibility.

"Always think positive," Jim would say. *"If you think positively, it will happen, not always, but most of the time. Got to go with the percentage."*

He was having a hard time thinking positively as of late, but he would always tell everyone else to do it.

Dawn was in the interview for thirty minutes. The entire time, Jim's thoughts went from extreme anger for choosing the profession he was in, to assassinations, to asking his Master and Spirit Guide for help in getting Dawn a job. Finally, she came out with a smile on her face.

"So, how did it go?"

"Really, really good. I believe I have a chance of getting it."

They were both excited as Dawn went over the entire interview with Jim on their return trip, expressing excitement about everything. She seemed very happy about the whole idea.

The next day, she got a call informing her that she had gotten the job and would have to come to the Harriette store to be trained for the first week before working in the Honsburg store. The trip and the gas it would take for a week were well worth the time and money for both of them. So they went to their coin jar, counted out all their change, went to the bank, and cashed it in for bills. Then, they carefully calculated the miles and the amount of gas they would need.

Dawn would work out very well for the video store owner and, in time, become very good friends with Allen Wesley. Her good looks, bubbling personality, and ability to communicate well with the general public allowed her to get the job. Her knowledge of bookkeeping and management was a decisive factor, and for Jim, learning that the owner was not from Honsburg or Reynolds County was a significant factor. No one had their hands around Allen's throat or crushing his balls, telling him to do what *they* wanted. Allen Wesley was a man of his own mind and could give a damn less about the powers in the town or, for that matter, Reynolds County. Politics, to Allen, was a destructive disease, and he made every effort not to catch it. He owed no one anything and was intent on keeping it that way.

The job would keep Jim home for the summer and allow him to work around his home on his usual summer projects to repair things. He was building this or that. Dawn always seemed to have a new idea for improving their house, whether inside or outside.

♉

Their summer went by quickly. Michael was home and worked for Kleeco Construction Company building bridges, learning how to tie steel, and using a jackhammer throughout his summer. Jim was incredibly proud of Michael, as he had always been a hard worker, striving to be the best at whatever he did.

When August came and the football players reported back for training, Michael did not go. He had decided not to play football in his second year of college. Instead, he wanted to play baseball in the fall and spring. He was more suited for the game of baseball and enjoyed it more. His roommate and friend Stacy opted for the more physical game of football. He was the most unlikely of the two to play football, even as a defensive back. His speed and height made up for his lack in bulk and weight, as he only weighed 170 pounds and had reached his final height of six feet one. Stacy's tall, lean frame, excellent hands, and ability to read QBs made him a perfect DB for a small private college.

Patrick would be entering his last year of junior high and was not overly excited about returning to school. However, Jim and Dawn were worried about him and his attitude toward education. They feared that his nightmare (to him at his age) experience would set him behind and that he would not rebound and get back on course.

Jim had been in contact with Dan intermittently throughout the summer, and Dan had encouraged him to get more involved in the teacher association business, political as it was. Jim loved the study of politics and loved to teach it but did not know if he was ready to get directly involved in the grand scheme of things, as he felt he had enough enemies as it was. But, of course, you make enemies quickly to get directly involved in the political game. So Jim weighed his options and figured he knew his enemies, so if he picked up a few more, it would not damage him more than they had already. But, on the other hand, he figured he could make some good allies if he could serve the politicians' needs and come in line like everyone else.

♉

According to Holly, his case was moving along as expected, and she would give him an update from time to time by letter or a rare phone call. He rarely had to go to her office; when he did, it was for a meaningful purpose. She was straightforward and to the point each time James Patrick met with her, something he liked. He felt good about Holly and thought that she could handle Damon well. Jim thought she knew how to play hardball with the best and probably better than most.

At one point in a meeting concerning her plan of operation, she asked, "Jim, are you aware of who you are suing?"

"Yes, I am."

"I really don't think you are."

He looked at her with puzzlement.

"You are not just talking about two lowlifes that have made your life miserable for the past … ever how many years now. No, you are about to take on the entire Democratic Party of Reynolds County. Now, don't sit there and look at me like that. You know who runs the county and that these people are connected to all the other power players in the county. So, you are smart enough to know that they will aid one of their good ole boys. Make no mistake about it; they will do whatever it takes to defend Damon. Richard, welll, he is along for the ride. Hell, if they could sacrifice him without any damage to their political comrade Damon, they would in a heartbeat. However, he could prove to jeopardize this case; too many connecting links so that they will carry him. They know that he would roll over on all of them in this case. Trust me on this one. I know you are not the trusting type, but I have done my homework, and I know, believe me!"

Jim started to speak, but she interrupted him.

"Hold your question. Are you aware that the Reynolds County School Board has agreed to pay for their attorney and all legal expenses?"

"No." His thoughts raced. "Now, wait one minute here, Holly. I mean, I ... I mean ... does that mean we can file a suit against the school board?"

"No."

"Why?"

"Because they did not write the letter."

"But—"

"No, but to it. They can foot his bill all they want. That does not mean they are directly involved. I just got through telling you what you are about to face. Now, do you want to carry this thing out to the end, knowing what you do at this point?"

Jim did not waver for a moment. "Yes!"

Holly continued. "You know there are no guarantees as things stand now."

"Yes, I am aware of that. My name has been tarnished. They leave me no choice. Either one defines one's name, or it is meaningless.

Now, do you think I have been damaged?"

"Yes, I do, and probably more than you even realize. A winning attitude is good. But bear in mind, things could and most likely will get rough before all is said and done. So, I want you to be aware of that right up front. There could be a lot of fallout from this, okay?"

"Okay."

"Do you have any questions?"

"Yes. I was about to ask if the school board's insurance will cover them."

"No, and I will give you two reasons. They know that Bales screwed up with his letter campaign against you. And this last one went over the line. Two, I think the major power brokers in the network over there asked them not to cover him. Now, before you ask, I will tell you. Because that would mean a larger sum of money, and, most likely, a jury would be more apt to award you a larger sum if you should win the case. And juries are more apt to find in favor of you if the insurance is picking up the tab. And believe me, they do not want you to win this case. The money is secondary. They are less likely to award you a large sum if it is just the two that the money is coming from."

Jim went into a total mood change almost at once.

"Jim, before you get too far down, and I can see it coming, your face gave you away. We can win this case. It is a good case, and you could get a good chunk of money out of this, but we have to face reality, like it or not, okay?"

He sat looking at his attorney. She had a very pretty face, and she was smiling. Her smile was warm and directed with a degree of confidence. It was not a fake smile he got from his colleagues all the time nor from some lowlife politician seeking his support during an election year who would not give him the time of day in between. He got no bad vibes from her, nothing telling him to be aware, no warning signals. She did not have to say another word. He saw and felt.

On the way home that day, he thought about what Holly had said about the Democratic Party. He had leaned toward the Democratic Party for the most part, although he was an independent voter. However, Holly belonged to the Republican Party. Jim did not reveal his political preference to her but knew he had no connections to any political party. He was just a single vote when they needed it. In addition, Jim and Dawn did not like everything either party stood for. So they based whomever they supported on the person, not the party line. Jim always felt that political parties were cults.

James P. once told me while we were engaged in a political discussion that to follow along with any party line was to sacrifice one's ability to think for oneself.

Langley Connection

It had been a week since "The Man" had made the call to the "castle." It was 10:00 p.m. Friday when the call came through on one of the three phone lines. Only two people had the number on his line that rang in his security office. When this phone rang, a reel-to-reel tape recorder would automatically click on. His den, located in his basement, had a large glass door leading outside to a large patio. The "man" spent much of his time in his den, where he often would read, watch television, or sit outside his lounge chair, enjoying the late afternoon and evening. His den had a large dark maple desk located toward the middle of the room, and on it was a phone, a laptop, a pencil holder, a legal tablet, and a square walnut box the size of a cigar box with a small rectangular red light at the end of the box. The light would flash when he received a call, letting him know that the "castle" connection had been activated. He then would enter his security room and call the number.

It was Sunday when he arrived back at his mountain retreat. As he went down to his den, he saw the light was on. He went to his high-tech "war room" and placed a call. It was 6:30 p.m. The phone rang twice and then connected.

"Hello."

"Age cannot wither her, nor custom stale." A short pause of silence was on the line.

"Her infinite variety."

"*Antony and Cleopatra.*"

"Act II. Scene 2."

"How are you doing?"

"Good, just playing the game." Then both laughed together.

"Ohhhh, yeahhhh … how well I know."

"What do you have for me?"

"46 degrees, 51 minutes 13 seconds N. latitude … 114 degrees 10 minutes 07 seconds W longitude … do you need a number?"

"Negative on that. We don't operate like that."

"Understood, it just disappeared."

"I thought you would."

"You know, this guy has got one hell of a service record."

"I know."

"Seems to be a little bit of a mystery surrounding it, my kind of man."

"Mine too, and you don't know the half ... really our kind of person. Remember that paper trails do not always tell the real story."

"Yes, I know, do I ever know ... ah, it is all that one wants to believe?"

"You are very much correct on that one."

"Say, I have some vacation time coming, and I was ..."

"Say no more. The fishing is good here. When can I expect you?"

"Let's say, ahh, ohhh, in forty-five from, let's see ... ahh, hell today."

"Sounds real good. It has been at least two years since I have seen you. Oh, is the pope traveling with you?"

"I suspect he will. You might as well count on it. Stock up on the beer."

"That is a done deal."

"Oh, how long will you be on this recon mission?"

"Shall we say seven?"

"Seven sounds like a good number."

"Got a few new gadgets for you. I think you will like them; they are good for listening."

"Anything new in commo?"

"Ohhh, yes. I would never leave you out on it. Haven't I always taken care of you?" Then more laughter.

"Affirmative on that."

"Look, as always ..."

"Yes, I will, and you also." Then click, as he hung the phone up.

He exited the security room, entered the den, and dialed a number.

On the other end of the line, a voice answered, "Hello."

"Andy, meet me in the office around 0900 hours tomorrow."

"Okay, will be there."

By noon Monday, Andrew was on his way to Montana. He touched down in Helena by late afternoon, picked up his rental car, and was in Missoula by 2100 hours, a hundred miles away. He checked into the preregistered Hampton Inn Hotel on North Reserve Street in the northernmost part of Missoula.

The following morning, Andy located the post office, and by 0900 hours Tuesday, he was inquiring about where he could locate J. Patrick O'Francis.

Jim was off helping and getting more education on running a ranch. A local rancher had befriended him, and Jim was getting another lesson on ranching in Montana.

His neighbor introduced himself because of the Masonic symbol on the back of Jim's truck window. Jim went over to his vast ranch that bordered his but was four times the size. He often went by and worked all day, learning an occupation he knew very little about from his oldest son, Bob Lewis III, who was in his late twenties. Jim learned that Bob Lewis II served in Vietnam and had a nice scar just below his left lower ribs, made by a round from an AK-47. The Masons and Nam would bond the two, making communication easy. Bob raised cattle and a lot of them. Jim had no problem being a student and learned quickly.

Just after 1800 hours, James P. returned home and had not much more than stepped from his truck when Andrew arrived. O'Francis did not have a clue as he saw the car approaching his home. He reopened the truck door and reached for his .357 in a holster on his seat. Jim waited for the approaching vehicle to come to a stop. He laid, "Mr. Smith and Mr. Wesson" on the edge of the seat and stood against the open door as he watched the car stop about twenty yards away. Andy had only delivered "mail" to James P. twice, which had been several years back when Jim was a teacher. On the other hand, Jim did not recognize the man casually getting out of his car. Jim noticed that he had a large brown envelope in his right hand. Seeing that, he knew "the Man" had tracked him down. James P. smiled. As Andy walked toward him, he thought it had to be extremely important, or he would not be getting "mail."

"Mr. O'Francis?" Andy addressed Jim.

"Yes, that would be me."

"Sir, I have a delivery for you. I have been instructed to tell you, and I quote, 'This did not take place. You are safe.'"

"Okay, I can live with that."

Andy handed him the envelope, turned, and began walking toward his car. Jim stood watching what he figured to be a man in his early to middle thirties, and just when he reached the car door he had left open, O'Francis spoke.

"Say there, would you answer me a question?"

Andrew paused with his right hand on the edge of the driver's door. "Sure, if I can."

Jim shoved the gun back in its holster, attached it to his left hip, closed his truck door, and walked toward Andy with the envelope in his left hand. "In all the years and of all the times someone has delivered one of these," and he held it up as if showing Andy as he continued to advance, "I have never asked anyone their name. Would you tell me your name?"

"Sure, Mr. O'Francis, my name is Andrew Jefferson Stone."

Jim smiled as he reached the car.

"Andy, have you had dinner yet?"

"Well, no, as a matter of fact, I have not. I just figured I would find a place in town to eat."

"If you have no objections, or I guess I should say if you can, would you like to join me for dinner?"

"I would like that, thank you."

"Good, let's get a drink, and I will tell my cook to put another plate on the table."

"Do you think it will be okay with her?"

"Well, her is him. And no, he will not mind." James Patrick just had to giggle. "No, nothing new in my life to have extra mouths at the dinner table. Do you drink? When Dawn was alive, she would fix dinner for any number of students on any given day. They never came to our home at feeding time and were not given a plate."

Jim giggled again and, with a warm smile, stopped and turned to face Andy. "You know, I think they always showed up at dinner just because Dawn was such a damn good cook."

"Does anyone call you A.J.?"

"A few people, not many."

As they entered the house, Jim introduced Broderick Carlson to his guest and informed him that he would be staying for dinner. The two men went to the great room.

B.C., as Jim referred to him, was an inspiring chef who worked at the Montana Club, breakfast through lunch, and on occasions prepared dinner. Jim hired him to cook dinner for him five days a week and was flexible with B.C.'s schedule. The extra job added to his income, which the twenty-six-year-old needed. He was not an Iron Chef yet, but he was good.

"Drink anything special, A.J.?"

"I usually like scotch, but... "

"No buts, you are in good company, unless you want a beer?"

"No-no, if you have scotch..."

"Oh, now *that* I do have, got some good Irish whiskey if you like?"

Later, after another fine meal prepared by Broderick, they spent a short time in some small talk, never bringing up any business.

Jim had retired to his great room shortly after Andy left. He sat in his rocking chair, looking out the front window as he opened the envelope. He removed the contents and began reading.

J. Patrick,

My apologies for intruding into your life. I think you need to be enlightened as to some events that could affect you.

I want you to know that I respect your semi-isolation and your new life, but I would never have located you if I felt that this was not of the most significant importance. And by the way, you hid well.

Joseph has contacted me, and he has asked me to locate you. He stated that it was imperative that he talk to you. And Jim, as of this letter, I have not notified him that I have located you. However, I am sending you a copy of a newspaper clipping concerning someone in your past life.

This will be your call. I will do what you wish. My courier will be staying at the Hampton Inn in Missoula. He will await your answer."

The phone rang in his living room.

"Hello."

"Sir, this is Andy."

"Did you have a good trip?"

"Sure did, and no hitches."

"Did you locate him?"

"Yes, sir. Sir, he asked me to stay for dinner. I hope you don't mind. I spent about three hours with him."

There was a short pause of silence.

"No problem. Well, his hospitality does not surprise me."

"He is a really nice person. We had a delightful evening. Sir, no business was discussed."

"That too does not surprise me, Andy."

"Politics, weather, and farming, or I guess ranching out here."

"Okay, you did well. He will contact you. Await his call, and you will be bringing an envelope back with you. And Andrew, you go to his place. Do not let him come to you, and he will insist, but tell him that you have your instructions, okay?"

"Yes, sir, no problem here."

"I'll see you in a couple of days." Then he hung the phone up.

Andrew got up early and had breakfast and several cups of coffee, awaiting his phone call.

Andy's phone rang at 10:00 a.m.

"A.J. Stone?"

"Yes, this is he."

"This is James Patrick O'Francis. I have an envelope for you to take back to your boss. I will be at your room in about thirty minutes."

"Mr. O'Francis, sir … I have been instructed to pick the envelope up from you at your place, sir." A pause.

"Okay, if that is the way he wants to do it."

"Yes, sir, it is. I can be there within the hour."

"Sure thing. I will have a cup of coffee for you. Oh, say, have you had breakfast?"

"Yes, sir, early."

"Well, you can have a good cup of coffee before you go. See you shortly."

♉

Andrew delivered the envelope back to Paul's office by midday Friday. Paul sat with his feet propped up on the windowsill, leaning back in his chair, looking out the window to the street below, something he liked to do, watching people, and his office was a perfect place to do just that. He opened the envelope and pulled out the letter.

"I am aware that you could find me with all your connections. I have no problem with you knowing my location, as I know I will remain lost (or I surely hope I am). Thank you for the news clipping, very interesting. And there was no remorse here! I did not ask for the job to be done. As to Joseph... I would like for you to inform him that I wish to remain 'lost.' I do not think he will have a problem with that. I will go as far as meeting him in Chicago if he needs to talk to me that bad. But I do not want anyone to know where I am! I will communicate through you and you only! No other way!

"Thank you for keeping my privacy private. I am enclosing my cell number. It, of course, has only a minimal number of people, and you have just made my shortlist. J. Patrick."

Janice Jones and her husband retired from teaching with an excellent retirement, as the last three years of one's working career are the basis for what you will get monthly on your retirement check. The school system had taken care of Janice, for she had been part of the "good ole boys" network. She had performed her duties well over the years, and she had been rewarded for her work. Her monthly paycheck was standard for the years in the profession, but the extra money she was awarded put her at the top pay in the county, from $40,000 per year, no matter how many years one taught, to a nice sum of $90,000 per year. Many people were aware of her "extra" pay for her "work," but none would do anything about it. She had damaged many, many students over her longevity in Reynolds County, but the job she had done on O'Francis was the one she was most proud of. An absolute masterpiece, one for the performing arts, an Oscar winner for sure. But her deeds and her performance would ultimately be put to the test. She and her co-conspirators had no idea as to the man whose character they had assassinated. They tarnished his family name and caused financial hardships for his family. At her end, she would have to ask herself, *was it worth the cost?*

Jordan Black

Jordan Black opened her eyes and blinked several times to get them focused as she viewed the mural ceiling. A collage of Native American scenes covered the entire ceiling over her queen-size hand-carved bed. The four large bedposts were of Native American busts, with the foot and headboards displaying carvings of Native American warriors on horseback, a spectacular piece of artwork.

She flipped the sheet and a light blanket to her right and rolled herself to the left and onto the hardwood floor. It was five-thirty in the morning, and the sun was just peeking its orange sphere up out of the gulf waters. Quintana Beach, just east of Freeport, Texas, was where she made her home, a two-story house designed to her specifications. It was located at the end of Quintana Drive, far enough away from the other residents to allow her a great deal of privacy. A two-car garage and a large storage area took up the first level.

There was no front entrance to Jordan's house. Instead, a set of stairs inside the garage allowed access into a small foyer off her kitchen. The only other doorway was to the back deck, which ran the entire length of the upper level, with one set of semicircular stairs at one end leading to a small backyard. Several hundred yards of dunes, wild grasses, and weeds small bushes dotted the area leading to the beach. She had purchased several acres surrounding her home, preventing anyone from building close to her. The beach stretched several hundred feet to the blue waters of the Gulf of Mexico. The house was set up high off the ground with reinforced concrete stilts to prevent flooding during the hurricane season or tropical storms that did not happen often, but her living quarters remained dry when it did. The three-bedroom, expensively furnished home had never been lost to the ravages of Mother Nature.

After relieving her blather of wastewater, she walked to the heavy double glass doors and walked out onto her deck. Placing her hands on the railing and leaning her golden-brown, fully naked body forward, tilting her head back and concaving her back, she felt the disks pop down her back, stretching her calves as she closed her eyes and sucked in the fresh morning air.

Jordan was a single forty-year-old who looked like she was maybe thirty, an attractive Native American Creek. She stood five feet five inches tall and weighed 125 pounds with an hourglass figure with near-perfect measurements, a firm body from the top of her head to the tip of her toes.

She was well educated, her bachelor's from the University of Texas in sociology, her master's from the University of Michigan in military history, and her Ph.D. from Georgetown in international terrorism.

Today is a good day to go fishing, she told herself. Returning to her bedroom, she made the bed, slipped on a pair of tattered-legged cutoff blue jeans, picked out an oversized T-shirt, gathered it up at the bottom, and tied a knot in it on her right side. Then she went down to the garage, slipped on her sandshoes, picked up her fishing gear, went to the storage area, got some fresh bait out of the refrigerator, opened the electric garage door, and walked her usual pathway to the beach.

While fishing, catching several, and tossing them back, Jordan went through every detail in the mind of her last contract. Satisfying herself that she had made no mistakes ultimately assured her that there had been no errors, and after three hours of fishing, she returned home. It was midmorning, and she was hungry. She got on her twenty-one-speed bicycle, pedaled out of her garage, turning and clicking the electronic door, closing it, which automatically set the alarm system. She traveled two miles to the small gulf town of Quintana. At 830 Lamar Street, she stopped at the Sand Bar and Grill. There she ordered a BLT special and socialized with the regulars.

No one knew a great deal about the attractive and sensual woman who regularly visited the Sand Bar. They knew she kept to herself, drove a silver BMW, rode her bike, fished off the beach as well as the pier, and made trips out of town for various periods. Jordan preferred it that way. From time to time, she would stop by the Sand Bar and Grill at night for a few beers and dance with a few locals with whom she was acquainted. Sometimes a male who was not acquainted with her would hit on her with flashes of a one-night stand cluttering his mind and would inevitably ask some feckless questions about what she did for a living. Jordan's usual response was that she was retired. Then, of course, the young stud with his testosterone in overload would press her for what she did before her retirement, hoping for a conversation that might lead to a bed. Of course, she would reply with a smile, "I was in the exterminating business."

Jordan never made those mistakes. No one came by her house, and she never dated or had any one-night stands with anyone from the area. A few drinks at the bar, a dance, and that would be it. Her personal life was hers. Her professional life was another matter altogether.

Jordan Black was born into a Creek family in Broken Arrow, Oklahoma, a proud Native American family dating back to Menewa or known to the "Indian" world as Hothlepoya *(Crazy War Hunter)* of the Lower Creek Nation.

Joseph and Martha Black had one daughter, White Star. But in the white man's world, they had been forced for generations to live with the white man's names. But to Jordan's Native American friends and close acquaintances, she was known as White Star. Those who were not within her circle thought it was just a nickname.

When she was twelve, Jordan's mother and father died in an automobile accident caused by three drunken, prejudiced, racist white supremacists in a pickup truck.

It had been a pleasant Saturday night as Joseph and Martha traveled back from their friend's house. Jordan was staying with her girlfriend, who was having a slumber party.

Hanging their heads out the window, yelling and driving wildly, the three drunken men played chicken with approaching vehicles, then swerved out of the way at the last possible moment or caused the approaching vehicles to veer off the road to avoid a head-on collision. The three men then would laugh and turn up another beer. The two-lane highway gently rose and dipped through the rural Oklahoma countryside like the open ocean tide. The moon was full, and the night sky was clear. The driver reached to his left and turned off the lights. As he did so, he drifted into the left lane. Approaching just to the opposite side of the rise in the road were Joseph and Martha Black. As their 1970 VW reached the top of the rise, it was met by a 1980 Chevrolet pickup. There had not been time for brakes to be applied nor to swerve out of the way. The oncoming sixty-mile-per-hour modified truck with its oversized tires and lift kit sheared the top of the small car off, instantly killing the two passengers.

Having no brothers or sisters, Jordan had been raised by friends of the Black family.

Jordan was brilliant and excelled in school. Her favorite sports were riding horses and shooting. The school had a rifle team, and Jordan was their best shot among both males and females. She continued her love of the sport in college and won many first-place awards with the rifle and the pistol.

She bid good night to her acquaintances at the local pub where she had eaten dinner and had a few beers. It was ten o'clock when she mounted her bike and started her two-and-a-half-mile trek to her apartment. Jordan was in her last semester of completing her master's, and she would be off to

Georgetown University by June. It was a typical April night in Ann Arbor, Michigan, cool, but Jordan liked it and liked riding her bike wherever and whenever she could. As she approached North University Avenue and Observatory Street, she slowed and observed no approaching vehicles. Making a left on Observation, she made her way to Washington Heights and turned right. Her mind drifted to her planned studies at Georgetown University and her Ph.D. She turned left onto North Hospital Drive but did not see the dark-blue 1993 Jaguar turning onto the same street until the last moment. Jordan swerved her bike to the left, but it was too late. She ricocheted off the left-front fender, losing her balance. She tumbled to the pavement. Anthony Scarola stopped his car, jumped out, and came to her aid. She was sitting up as he approached her.

"Are you all right?"

She paused and looked up at the very handsome six-foot-one, black-haired, brown-skinned man.

"Yes, I think so." Then, as he reached his right hand out toward her, she reached up and took it, and he helped her to her feet.

"I am so sorry. I didn't see you. Did I damage your car?"

Anthony had not looked. It did not matter to him, as it was a piece of metal with four wheels. Expensive, yes, but money for Anthony Scarola was not a problem. Anthony looked at her bike and saw its front wheel was warped.

"Looks as if your bike is damaged," he stated, and Jordan looked over at it lying a few feet from her.

"Shit! Oh, sorry. I did not—"

Anthony cut her off. "No problem, I've used much worse. Look, ahh, may I take you somewhere?"

Jordan paused before answering. "Ahh—"

Anthony Scarola could see the concerned look on her face. It was late, and she had no clue as to who he was. "Look, Miss—" He paused.

"Jordan," she responded.

"Jordan, I can put your bicycle in the trunk, and I will be more than glad to drop you wherever."

"Well, okay. It isn't far, just to North Nichols."

Anthony picked up the bike, popped open the trunk, and maneuvered the back wheel into it, leaving the better part of the bike sticking out. Jordan was waiting by the passenger's door. Anthony walked to the door, opened it, and gestured with his left hand to get in. In a matter of minutes, they arrived at her apartment. Anthony removed the bike from the trunk.

"Do you need any help?" he inquired.

"No thanks, I can get it. But look, Mister, ah—" Then she paused for a moment. "I don't know your name."

"Anthony Ryan Scarola. No, Mister." Jordan stuck her hand out, and Anthony shook it.

"Anthony, if you would give me your address, I will pay for the damage to your fender."

Scarola smiled, reached into his inside jacket pocket, pulled out a pocket planner, opened it, took a business card out, and handed it to Jordan.

"Call me when you get a chance. And Jordan, don't worry about the fender."

He turned, walked by the trunk, closed it, got in the Jag, and drove off.

Two days later, a twenty-one-speed bicycle, a much more expensive one than Jordan had, along with a basket of flowers, was delivered to her apartment with a note.

"Hope this will do. Sorry for the inconvenience. Give me a call."

Sign, Anthony Ryan Scarola.

Anthony was born in New York in 1958. He graduated from NYU with a degree in business. Then he attended Boston University for his master's in financial analysis. His success was measured in his wealth, not that of his family.

Joseph Antonio Scarola, Anthony's father, was born in New York in 1933. He had been very successful in his business of distributing liquor to stores, bars, pubs, and hotels. Joseph Antonio was the son of Joseph Michael Scarola, born in Italy, and immigrated to the United States in 1927, where he worked on the docks as a dockworker. He would become a boss and a major player in running one of New York's largest docks.

Anthony Ryan Scarola's mother, Mary Catherine Ryan, was the daughter of Logan Kendrick Ryan. His Irish family had arrived in Boston in 1930. Mary Catherine's father went into the bar business and became one of the largest bar owners in the Boston area over many years. Mary Catherine became a nurse and left Boston for New York. She met Joseph Antonio Scarola when he was brought into the hospital for treatment after an accident occurred on the dock where he was working.

Mary and Logan's son Anthony would become Vincent Spadolini's accounting department head of his large shipping business.

Paul O'Neill

Paul picked the phone up and dialed a number. The phone rang three times before the pickup.

"Caprotti residence."

"Joseph, Paul here."

"Good morning, Paul." After some pleasantries, the conversation got to business.

"Good news, I hope?"

"Well, Joseph, yes and no."

"Okay, give me the good news."

"I did locate Jim."

"Okay, and ..."

"And ... well, Joseph ... he wants to remain, let's say, lost." There was another long pause in the conversation.

"Did you talk to him?"

"Yes, in a way. Yes."

"What exactly does that mean?"

"It means I have contacted him."

"Are you going to tell me where he is?"

"No. I won't do that."

"Look ..." Joseph started to insist.

"No, Joseph. Listen to me. He will come to Chicago if you want him to. But... he does not want to be found. Now, I can understand that, and so can you."

"Okay, okay, so you can contact him?"

"Yes, I can contact him."

"So ... okay ... how about this: let him know I need him to come to Chicago. You have my address. Let's say..." Joseph opened a daily planner. "Ahh, let's see... how about next month, ah, let's say Friday the twenty-second."

"Okay, I can tell him that. If he so agrees and makes the trip, how about, you meet him at the airport?" Paul asked.

"That will work. Tell him to plan on spending a couple of days or so with me. Then, tell him that Michael and I will be at the airport to pick him up."

"He will stay at your place?" Paul inquired for information.

"Ahh, yeah, he can stay here. Do you think he will need any money for the flight?" Joseph asked.

"I do not know that. I can handle the cost for him."

"Okay, tell you what, I will reimburse you for any costs. Fair enough?"

"Fair enough. I'll get back to you to confirm the yay or nay and the flight number and time of arrival." Paul replied. Then the line clicked and a dial tone. Paul kept the phone to his ear for several seconds and then hung up.

It was 2100 hours when Jim's phone rang. He let it ring, and after the fourth ring, the default answering voice informed the caller to leave a number and a short message and that a return call would come as soon as possible. Jim was sitting in his rocking chair to the left of a warm fire in his large rock fireplace, reading a book by Robert Parker and enjoying a few drams of Irish whiskey.

He put the book on the floor, got up, went to the kitchen, and looked at the phone number. He did not recognize it, so he clicked the recorded message. It was a short message. *"Sit-Rep."* Jim knew the code. He needed to talk to him.

He pulled out an obscure list of numbers, ran his finger down the page, and found the number he had been instructed to call. After the third ring, a voice answered with the letters, "*OSS.*"

Jim responded with, "*Wild Bill.*"

Then came the response, "*General William J. Donovan.*"

"Hey, how are you doing? It's been a long time." Paul stated.

"Guess you received my," then J. Patrick stopped himself as he realized it was a rhetorical question because "the Man" would not have called him if he had not received his letter. Then, Jim heard a laugh on the other end of the line.

"Yes, yes, it is good to hear your voice. I assume you are well and enjoying your new life."

"As well as can be for me. I can assume you are calling concerning our mutual friend?"

"Yes, he wants you to come to Chicago on the twenty-second of next month if at all possible." A pause lasted several seconds, and Paul waited in silence.

"Well, I think I can make arrangements."

"Will you need help financially?" Another pause for several more seconds. Then Paul spoke, "Not to trouble yourself. It will be covered."

"By whom?" James Patrick asked.

"By Joseph."

"How long of a stay?" Jim inquired.

"I do not know. I would expect two, maybe three days. Listen, when you make the flight, do not make it direct."

Another pause occurred while Jim thought.

"Of course, I understand. Do you have any suggestions?" Another pause in the conversation for a good ten seconds.

"Let me set it up for you, if you do not mind, that is?"

"No, no, I do not mind at all."

"I will handle the financing of the entire trip. It will be settled up at a later date."

"Well, ahh—"

"Look, don't worry. Our friend will reimburse me for all costs. Don't say a word. He can handle it with pocket change, and you know it! Forget pride on this one! Let me change the subject. I want to come to visit for a day or two if you do not mind. We need to do some talking face-to-face, okay?"

"Yes, I understand. On the subject of a visit by you, no problem. I would love to see you. Yes... I think that is a grand idea. I am so glad I thought of it," James P. stated. Then he laughed real big. Both began to laugh, one that reached down deep into both men, a rare moment of hearty laughter.

"Our friend told me you would stay at his place, no hotel."

"Why?"

"Why what, Jim?"

"Why his home?"

"Can't answer that for sure. Just have to speculate."

"Okay, let's hear it." Then a very quick, "No, no, no!" Came the quick response from Jim. "Let's not. This is a phone. Let it go. I can figure. But, hell, I am not stupid. I have been there and done that."

"I know you have. But I do not think there is a problem, let's say, higher up?" Paul stated.

"Okay. I was wondering just that. Have you met him?" Jim asked.

"Yes, many years ago. He is a very nice man, but all business. Make no mistake about that. Very upfront; pulls no punches. You should have no problems in that area. Just be you, and you two should hit it off very well. You don't have to be on guard. Tell it like it is and trust me on this. He would prefer it that way and does business that way. Jim, if you are not completely at ease with the offer, I will tell him you need to think about it, and we can talk when I come out. Keep in mind, this is my area of expertise, and I can be of service to you if you want. Think of it as baseball, no clock, just innings. No time limit."

"I thank you, and I may very well do just that. I do respect your skills. I will ask for advice on the matter if that is what this is all about." Jim stated.

"I don't think the events that have taken place are the subject. It is the future events that are the subject. I think it is your call that will be the subject," Paul responded.

"Okay."

"I'll have your flight plans to you in a few days."

"Good deal, thanks."

"No problem, thank you." And then they hung up.

Teachers' Association

Bobby Simms came to Mr. O'Francis' room and asked to talk to him for a few minutes. James P. stepped out in the hall, and in a short conversation, he learned that he needed his help for the following year's curriculum, as he had learned that they would change what was to be taught on the sixth-and seventh-grade levels. That afternoon, after school, he met Bobby in his office to discuss the matter. Simms informed him that they wanted to replace world geography with world history in the sixth grade. Jim objected to the idea, as he explained that the course was too deep for that age group. Furthermore, that age of students would not understand, and it could not be watered down enough for them to get it. He asked Bobby why the change, but he could not give him an answer.

"Well, Mr. O'Francis, what would you suggest?"

"Well, sir, I think that sixth graders should have the sequel to the US history that they are having in the fifth grade, and then give them world geography in the seventh."

"Why world geography instead of world history?"

"Because, Mr. Simms, world G. can be brought down to the seventh-grade level, and it can be made more interesting to the student. They can use it in high school in several course areas."

"For instance?" Bobby inquired.

"Okay. It can be used in US history, as the United States was involved in events in history throughout the world. They would be able to identify where these places are, Mr. Simms, as I have stated before, and, as you are aware of my statements, you cannot teach history without geography. They will, of course, be able to use it in world history or world geography, as it is their option to take as a freshman or sophomore."

"I like it, good sound reasons. I will do what I can to get this done. I will most likely need you to sit on a committee for adopting a textbook."

"Yes, sir, I have done that and will do it again if you ask me to do so."

"Thank you, Mr. O'Francis, and I will let you know."

Jim was having a difficult time figuring the kindness. Many years earlier, his suggestions were considered a joke and were laughed at. *Something is not fitting correctly. Now, what is it?* He went on his way home for the day. *Could it be that he has seen the light? Is it because Decal does not influence him? Was it Decal all along? Was Bobby Simms controlled that much by Decal? Did Simms realize that he was wrong about me and now wants to make amends? I cannot be fooled again by an act of good faith. He is a good-natured person. I want to trust him at this point in my career, but so much damage has been done. What about his connection to Damon? I know he and Marshy hate each other, and I cannot blame Simms for his dislike of Marshy. That is a plus. However, is Simms beginning to think independently and not listening to the ones that wish to destroy me and my career even further? I will not be fooled again. I will have to play this game out to the end, make no mistakes, and hope for the best.*

Damon arrived at Marshy's office at four o'clock. Already present were Duncan Brewer and Barnard Theodoric, the school board member from the Honsburg area whose usual occupation was that of a local drug pusher (pharmacist). All three were anti-O'Francis people, but they were churchgoing Christians. LaMar was a deacon in his church, and Barnard was a Sunday school teacher.

After a two-hour session, it was agreed that Damon Bales would retire at the end of the year. He was leaving the system as payment for all the legal fees that would accrue in the future. Bales had been adamant about O'Francis being fired from his teaching job, and the three "big political dogs" assured him that they were working on it and that he would be gotten rid of.

After Damon left, the three men continued their conversation concerning Damon and O'Francis. Barnard asked LaMar if he could get O'Francis fired from his teaching position. LaMar assured him that it could be done. He informed the other two that he was told Bobby Simms would take the early-retirement plan offered, and his replacement was to be Scott Wolffe.

Duncan spoke at that point. "I can assure you, Barnard that he can get the job done. He has already been briefed on the matter, and he is the man for the job. He won't take any of O'Francis' bullshit. He worked for us before and will set his goddamn ass up! He will not leave any loose ends for him to squirm out on!"

Theodoric shook his head. "I don't know, do not forget about Jakes."

Marshy was quick in his response. *"Fuck Jakes! That sonofabitch!* Scott has been told by God, and he had damn sure better do his job. He says he had people who would help him. I'm getting damn tired of O'Francis. He's been a damn pain in the ass for too damn long! If Bales had not gotten so damn personally involved and let O'Francis get to him, he could have!"

Duncan interjected, "With our help."

"Yeah, we damn sure would have had to help him, but shit, he and Richard blew it!"

Theodoric asked, "Did you ever find out how he was getting his info? I mean, it appears to me that he seems to know what we are going to do before we do it."

LaMar angrily got up from his chair. "Shit! I don't know. I have checked and rechecked, and it ain't any of our people, and I know that for a fact! Hell, I even had professional people come in here and check for bugs! I had the phone lines checked just to make sure."

LaMar's voice rose with the thought of O'Francis still in the system.

Theodoric rose and stretched. "LaMar, just what did he do to you?"

LaMar cut his question off. "By God, the sonofabitch supported that dump-ass ole man, Henry Marwin, for one thing! And for another, he caused me many problems over that damn baseball field up at Honsburg. Hell, I know he was the one who got the damn newspaper involved, by God. I have my sources. He seems to know just a little too damn much about the flow of money and some of the connections we have. And another thing, I never did like the bastard way back when I had a brief baseball season with him."

Barnard had a puzzled look on his face. "What do you mean by playing baseball with him?"

"Oh, hell, I don't remember ... ahh back in ... maybe the summer of '68, we played on a baseball summer team together. First time I met him. Then he left the area, and I wish the sonofabitch had stayed gone. I guess if it had not been for dumbass Don Morgan, hell, he would have... but at any rate, I just didn't like his cocky nature. Hell, I guess he was in some special type of army unit or some shit, or that is what I was told at one time. It didn't matter a damn to me what he was in, he... well, I just didn't like him! Asked too damn many questions, won't go along with the game plan, and won't come in line like everyone else. Unfortunately, it appears that no one can bring him in line! Is that enough reason for you?"

"Well, I remember him in high school," Theodoric began. "And I had to play basketball against him, and I damn sure didn't like him! Bubble-gum-blowing showoff bastard. Shit, I don't know anyone who liked him on our team. So, we talked about putting him out of the game if we ever got the chance."

"Well, did you?" LaMar asked with a slight grin on his face.

"Ah, hell no, we would knee him, run him into the wall, and he still kept going!"

Duncan interrupted. "Look, all that shit is in the past! Now we have a chance to get him out of the system. He creates too much trouble, not just with the students but also with parents and our operation, which is the essential item we should be concerned with. School shit can be handled. I still worry about why he has not gone public or even tried to blackmail us. I am telling you he knows about all of it. That should worry both of you. He can get information about what we do, and how it is done is an even more significant concern for me. Another thing, now, boys, I am telling you, if he gets involved in that goddamn association shit, he will be a real pain in the ass. Until now, I understand he has been out of all the internal workings and the political part of the teachers association.

"I am telling you! If he gets intertwined into the political aspect of the political system outside of this county, we can't handle it. We can control our people, but beyond that, well... we have enough problems now with a few of the damn radical teachers spread throughout the county. As far as I can tell, it appears that none knows a damn thing about our operation. Hell, they ain't, but about a half dozen and we damn sure don't need O'Francis getting involved, especially if O'Francis starts talking about matters outside the teaching profession. Most of these people can be handled. They are scared to death anyway. If he can't be brought in line, we will get rid of him, which is the bottom line. Once that is done, he will just leave, which is what we want. LaMar, you will give him an excellent recommendation to wherever, but away from around here! Here, LaMar means far away. Not just a county or two over. That will be it. We can get on with business without any worries."

After a short pause, no one was talking.

"Shit, LaMar," Duncan continued, "you know very well how to get it done, and you have people that will work with you. Decal made sure that he established his rep in the coaching area. All we have to do is stir it a little, and the rest will take care of itself. At least someone did get something on him that we could make damn sure will continue to cause him problems. He has no chance of getting a job anywhere close. You will have the board behind you, and you know it. Bring him up on some type of bullshit charge, and they will take care of the rest. All this talk about killing him is bullshit. Damn it, you know damn well, that will bring too much heat, especially on our friend on the court, not to mention our prosecuting attorney connection. I mean... damn, boys, if it wasn't for good old Douglas... well, of course, I don't want to forget Trooper Penrod, but... shit... if Douglas had not been the Commonwealth, if he had not been where he was or if it had been some of our not-so-good friends, we would have been fucked!"

Duncan was in total command of the room.

"There are too many other things at stake here. I mean, we have some people depending on us to make money for them. Now, I do not have to tell you these people are not the ones to be messed with. We have all enjoyed the ... shall I say, the fruits of our little tree. I personally am one who is not going to kill the fruit tree. If, and I mean *if*, things get too far out of hand with O'Francis, we can always let these people know, and they will handle the matter."

The entire room was deathly silent. Duncan took a drink of coffee.

"That is if they have to get involved. We will not have anything to do with it. There will be no connection to the school system or any of its personnel whatsoever. They can do these things better than we can."

Dan called and asked Jim to meet him at St. Pete for a pre-caucus meeting for the upcoming VEA convention, to see how things worked and start to get a feel for what the association was about. He would introduce him to some of the officers and some of the more active people in other counties that were to be present, including the people from Richmond.

James Patrick arrived at 1745 hours and talked to several teachers he knew, including a person he had not seen since childhood. Emmanuel Reuben had been a boy who hung around with the "big boys" during his youth, a mosquito that buzzed around the older teens, very likable, but for an older teen, a mosquito. The first thing Jim recalled when he recognized Emmanuel was one of their sandlot football games. Jim was the quarterback, and Emmanuel would attach himself to Jim like a leech to his leg or back and hang on for dear life while O'Francis scrambled to get his pass off. Each time a play ended, he would tell one of his teammates, "Keep that little shit off me!" However, to no avail, the "little shit" seemed to manage to get by the big boys and attach himself to O'Francis in one form or another.

When Jim and Emmanuel relived the good old days of childhood innocence, they laughed a good healthy, warm, loving laugh, which led to another story. *"Oh yeah, do you remember ..."* and then another story. After the meeting concluded, they stood outside as Reuben had a cigarette. Another funny story emerged as they had worked their way to the parking lot. It had been a very good reunion, something O'Francis had not expected. As Emmanuel stood by James O'Francis' car in the semi-darkness of the lower parking lot, smoking a cigarette, a car passed them, leaving the parking lot.

Emmanuel pointed to the car. "Do you know that person?"

Jim quickly looked at the car and did not recognize the auto now pulling out onto the street. He had a clear view of the car as the streetlights gave off enough light, but he did not recall the car or who may have been driving it.

"I do not believe I know the person, or I should say I do not recognize the car. Why?"

"Well ... I hate to spoil a good evening, but I feel you should know something."

O'Francis' smile left his face as his defensive system went up like a flashing meteorite piercing the night sky. His face turned stern and emotionless as he looked at the onetime childhood acquaintance.

Emmanuel's older brother Lance was Jim's age, maybe a couple of years older. Jim could relate to growing up with older boys. He had experienced the same thing and was sure that his onetime playmates, who were all older than he, felt at times that he too was a pain in the ass. Tagging along, aggravating them, emulating everything they would do and say.

Emmanuel was well aware that Jim had grown up with his brother, and he felt that he was a friend to Jim, even though there was a six-year difference between them.

Emmanuel looked at O'Francis in the pale light of the parking lot and could tell that he no longer had his "happy face."

"Look, I guess there is only one way to say this, and that is just to tell it like it is."

James P. still had not responded.

"Ah, that person approached me while you and Dan were talking and told me that I would be wise not to have anything to do with you. If I got involved with you in any manner, you would cause me a lot of problems; that you were nothing but trouble. You have big problems with all administrators that you worked for, and that your reputation was bad, and that being associated with you would give me a bad name. Now, do you know Sabrina Wagner?"

Jim turned his head quickly toward the road as if to see the car that had been gone for several minutes and then turned back to look at Manuel.

"Is that who that was?"

Emmanuel dropped his cigarette and crushed it out with his right foot.

"Yes, that is who was in that car."

Jim reached inside his sports jacket and pulled out a cigar, slowly licked the cigar from one end to the other, then took out a cigar cutter and clipped off the tip of it. Manuel stood and watched, saying nothing.

Jim lit his lighter, holding it to the end of the cigar for a few seconds, and then put it into his mouth. Then, drawing heavily on it until the end of the cigar glowed with fire and large puffs of smoke exhaled from his mouth, he continued to look at Emmanuel.

"Well ... Emmanuel, I guess it will be your call on this one. I can say nothing as to what you should or should not do."

Manuel reached into his shirt pocket, pulled out a pack of cigarettes, took one out, and lit it. Then, as he replaced the pack in his pocket, he spoke in a stern voice. "I will pick and choose who I associate with, and I will not choose my friends based on what someone else says about them."

They stood looking at one another.

"I mean what I say, Jim."

"Okay, I have no problems with what you are saying. However, I do want to tell you that if Wagner has anything to do with this association, as I can assume at this point she does, then ..." He stopped.

"I will leave it at that, Manuel. I appreciate you telling me. It was honorable of you. Thank you. Let's call it a night."

Jim turned and walked to his car. Manuel got in his car, and they departed.

James P.'s thoughts were on many events that had occurred over the years, and he could not

understand why people of Serbian's nature were
allowed to disrupt the lives of other people who had
really done nothing to them.

He had not been around her in many years and
had not known of her activities. But at that moment,
he figured that she had not been still. He figured that
her connections were with the same circle that preyed
on the weak and manipulated people into believing
everything they said as gospel. Oh, how the evil
disciples worked the Good Book and cloaked
themselves in righteousness.

O'Francis had not known for sure, however,
had suspected that she was working with the people
who were out to do him in.

☿

Time would tell as he would get involved in the
teaching profession's political scheme. He would not
throw caution to the wind because of a childhood
acquaintance. But, on the other hand, his feelings
were to give this old acquaintance a chance. His inner
alarms had not gone off while in the presence of
Manual. He heard no voices warning him of any
danger. So, he would move with prudence with

Manuel, letting time and events take their course. He would judge him on his actions, not his words.

As to Sabrina Wagner and the inner circle, she was embroiled, people like Jim O'Francis, he absorbs the pain of learning, and then he adjusts and overcomes it, for there is nothing more dangerous to unscrupulous humans than someone who knows their past. As time moves forward and lessons learned, and knowledge gained, the intended action is to remove the threat or enact revenge.

♉

Epilogue

James Patrick O'Francis' story is far from being over.

His fight to preserve his name and defend the students he taught was an ongoing battle.

He had become known as a student's teacher.

His adversaries never stopped coming after Jim and his family. What his nemesis did not understand was that James P. was a winner. He did not have the word *quit* in his DNA. When he was wrong, he admitted it. When he was right, he would fight.

Jim could not be intimidated. The minor threats were meaningless until they became a reality, and then it would be James Patrick's turn.

His enemies did not or could not accept or understand the makeup of a person like O'Francis. They could not conceive that if he lost his means of making a living for his family, he would levy an act of revenge they could not in their worst nightmares imagine. For James P. O'Francis, there was no time limit. They would be held accountable for their actions.

Songs and Lyrics used in this novel:
Smiling Faces, Sometimes:
Singing Group: The Temptations
Songwriters: Norman Whitfield &
Barret Strong

CHRISTINE JANE COUNTS O'CONNOR

"You ask how much I need you; must I explain?

I need you, oh my darling, like roses need rain.

You ask how long I'll love you; I'll tell you true:

Until the twelfth of never, I'll still be loving you."

Song by: Johnny Mathis: Lyrics by: Jerry Livingston and Paul Francis Webber:

J. Michael O'Connor